Travelling Cat
in Ireland

By the same author
Travelling Cat

Travelling Cat in Ireland

Frederick Harrison

HarperCollins*Publishers*

HarperCollins*Publishers*
77–85 Fulham Palace Road
Hammersmith, London W6 8JB

Published by HarperCollins*Publishers* 1991
9 8 7 6 5 4 3 2 1

A catalogue record for this book
is available from the British Library

ISBN 0–246–13700–2

Set in Bembo by
Falcon Typographic Art Ltd

Printed in Great Britain by
Scotprint Ltd., Musselburgh

For Hilda Harrison née Connolly

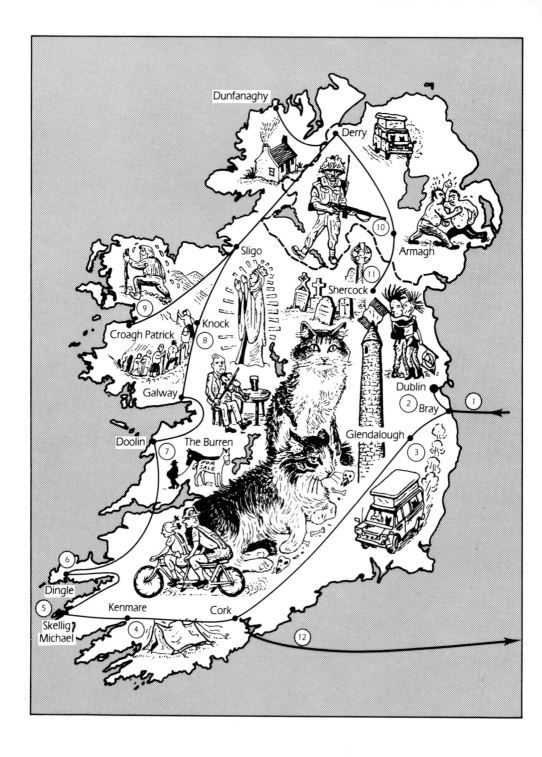

CONTENTS

1

The Sap Also Rises

'You have to admit, it's a beautiful day,' I said to my two travelling companions as we navigated the early morning streets of London and headed for the contra-flow purgatory of the M1. 'Don't you just love that sense of release, that liberation of the spirit, that expansion of time and space all journeys should begin with?'

Nothing. My fellow travellers were flaked out, dead to the world and to the joy of being on the road. Cats, of course, are creatures of routine and territory and it was, after all, another hour to sunrise. Not for them the subtle pleasures of the unknown. They go by their own clock, and 6AM means sleep, even when your territory is moving north at a steady 50 mph.

As the streets began to snarl with the daily grind of commuters Pugwash and Cheesy snoozed on. We were on our way to Ireland to spend the first spring and summer of the new decade exploring a country that was both known and unknown; and to get away for a while from a country that seemed to be losing its way.

While Pugwash was a veteran of the road, Cheesy was a veteran of the street, a subtle difference that was likely to dominate the power politics of the camper over the next six months. Given her personal habits and temperament – a feline pit bull terrier would not be stretching a point – you may well wonder why she was there at all. I know I did. The short answer is that long-suffering friends, scarred, battered and traumatized by occasional weekends of Cheesy-minding, had issued an ultimatum.

'There is no way I'm looking after that bloody cat for six months,' was the general gist of the response.

'Let's face it,' said one, an American friend who works with severely disturbed adolescents, 'that feline is definitely out to lunch.' They had a point.

Pugwash, son of Cheesy, was another matter. If ever a cat was made for the supposedly Caring Sharing Nineties, it was this one. People actually ring up to volunteer their cat-minding services for Pugwash. Maybe his Gandhi-like aura might rub off on his batty mother after a while. And then again, maybe not.

Surprisingly, the long haul to North Wales was uneventful – inside the camper van, that is. Outside was a different matter. The Welsh, too, have their own version of contra-flows which seemed to extend the entire length of the sadly ravaged coast that industry and commerce have hacked and scarred over the years. There was no redemption on arrival at Holy Island, either. I missed the ferry to Dublin by fifteen minutes and spent a long, aimless evening in the tacky little resort of Holyhead, which is unredeemed by the frisson of true seediness, and certainly not by the melancholic poetry of some coastal resorts off-season.

Gradually, the terminal's car-park began to fill with vehicles for the early morning ferry. With them came the first inkling of trouble. Virtually every car carried a dog, and a regular cacophony of barks and yelps swept across the car-park as one mutt after another was taken for walkies. None of this was lost on my two reprobates. With each wave of noise both Pugwash and Cheesy expanded with territorial rage behind the firmly locked windows of the van. Cheesy in particular was in her element, standing on her hind legs on the driving seat and vociferously offering to take on all comers in a fair imitation of Ceausescu in his farewell appearance on a Bucharest balcony. I had a sinking feeling there was about to be a similiar outcome, as a van drew alongside containing several large dogs and a sticker proclaiming 'Rottweilers do it in the road'. Terrific. As the canines peered balefully across the no-man's-land between us, both Pugwash and Cheesy paraded ostentatiously about. So much, then, for Pugwash as a moderating influence. The dogs went into such a frenzy that their van shook and rattled and bounced up and down. Their owner, a large sombre man of the kind who stand outside discos in dinner jackets and hit people for a living, stared steadily across at me, presumably seduced by his own mythology. I gave him a friendly smile – wouldn't you? – and breathed a deep sigh of relief as the tannoy announced it was time for loading.

With the Incorrigibles fed and locked securely in the hold, it was time to relax. I stood on deck and watched with mixed feelings as the dark outline of the neon-spangled land slid below an horizon that cradled the emblematic full moon. I would be gone for six months and the last fortnight had been spent saying fond and regretful farewells. I had a sense that something was passing but I was damned if I knew what. Maybe all journeys begin with a sense that something irretrievable is being left behind, if only because travelling changes perceptions of what has been left. On the other hand, I would be travelling in a strange country which, thanks to the political situation, seemed familiar. Everyone I knew had an opinion on Ireland, although few seemed to know much about it and fewer still had actually been there. Even the most perceptive of friends were likely to fall back on stereotypes when talking about the Irish. I found myself making a conscious effort to unload the accumulated baggage of impressions stretching back over several decades.

I also had a personal reason for examining Ireland first hand. My mother's side of the family, the Connollys, had originally come from the west coast, and meandered north before joining Ireland abroad. For some time I had felt a strong pull to retrace that journey, although I found it difficult to be specific as to why. Perhaps I had reached that age when it becomes imperative to look back in order to see what the future might bring.

Inside, the soporific environment of the ferry was untroubled by the 'earwego' brigade now endemic to the European cross-Channel routes. Sleep was everyone's priority. There was something oddly touching and vulnerable about the scattered bodies, curled foetus-like, lost in themselves and their dreams; the silence broken only by the reassuring heartbeat of the ship's engine.

From the deck the light of Howth Head could finally be seen, flashing intermittently on the horizon. The dawn of St Patrick's Day saw the grey of the sky blending seamlessly with the grey-green of Dublin Bay, its famous snot-green colour a matter of light perhaps, and the imagination of its home-grown writers, filtered through the prism of self-imposed exile. Down in the hold two slightly seasick cats glared at me accusingly as I drove off the ferry. The inevitable customs choice between nothing to declare and something brought

Two innocents abroad in a strange land . . . that made three of us

the usual twinge of guilt, in this case prompted by two sulking, bad-tempered cats.

'Anything to declare now?' asked the friendly customs man.

'No. Unless I need to declare . . . these two.'

'Will you look at this,' he said to no one in particular. 'I've never seen anything like that before.'

Looking at the raddled pile of thoroughly-pissed-off Cheesy, I could see his point.

'You'll be needing our man from the Agriculture,' said the customs man perceptively, calling him over. Details taken and formalities completed, our man peered more closely at the Ceausescu of the cat world. I just knew.

'Has it been in a fight a something?' said our man as he moved incautiously to stroke a primed Cheesy.

'I wouldn't do that if I were –'

'Whaaaargh!'

I extracted Cheesy gingerly from the Agricultural man.

'The focking thing bit me!'

'I know. I'm sorry. I think she's a bit disorientated.'

'Disorientated! The focking thing's lethal!'

More details, a lot more, were taken and eventually we left. Tempers ran a little high as I drove into Dublin. Mine did anyway.

'So much for a low-profile entry into Ireland. Our first day and well and truly dropped in it. Thanks a bunch, guys.'

Two sets of ears defiantly pointed the other way as the Incorrigibles took an unnaturally keen interest in a passing cloud.

I parked on the north side of the O'Connell Bridge by the side of the Guinness-black Liffey. London does its best to ignore the Thames and generally regards it as an inconvenience. Dublin has shaped itself around its famous river and made it a part of its mythology, even though, as local legend has it, 'the fastest way to get a hospital bed in Dublin is to fall in the Sniffy Liffey'. I took the precaution of feeding both cats before I left – even my two zonk out if you feed them enough. And with Cheesy on board there was little to fear from a break-in: Ireland's one and only Guard Cat.

O'Connell Street was a mass of tricolour bunting, primed and ready for the big parade. Ranks of empty seats by the world's best-known post office awaited the substantial forms of Dublin's leading citizens. In one of the more successful attempts at cross-fertilization that link Ireland with America, the St Patrick's Day parade in Dublin was imported from Boston and particularly New York – which has a larger Irish population than Dublin – in the early seventies to help promote tourism. Two hours later several hundred thousand Dubliners and friends had followed the hallowed Irish tradition of transposing reality into myth as they enthusiastically lined the streets to watch the blessing of the shamrock and cheer an exuberant display of Irish pride that took three hours to pass. Religion and politics aside, the Irish can never resist a party, and, in this case, something more fundamental was going on: a riotously joyful and uninhibited celebration of spring awakening. That the sap was rising was underlined when a battalion

A battalion of cheerleaders gave a display of synchronized safe sex . . .

of American pubescent cheerleaders in bright green ra-ra skirts gave
an enthusiastic display of synchronized safe sex to the ranks of local
dignitaries and churchmen. Exactly what that did for the libidos of
several life-long celibate custodians of the guilt-without-sex tradition
is not known. But well into my second day of celibacy, it certainly
cheered me up. I watched the parade feeling like Cecil Parkinson
on royal jelly, which was something Charlie Haughey, the rather
weary-looking Taoiseach, might have benefited from as he took the
salute. Standing next to him during the blessing of the shamrock
I heard him mutter 'Will you get a move on for fock's sake' to a
nervous young man who turned out to be both the Lord Mayor of
Dublin and his son. Keeping it in the family is another hallowed
Irish tradition, as is patriarchy, apparently. The Taoiseach is careful,

what this did for the libidos of Dublin's Finest is not known

however, to meet his electorate's expectations of a man of the people and although he looked, as well-known public figures invariably do in the flesh, like a wax model of himself, he was accessible to the crowd in a way that would be unthinkable in Britain and most other European countries. 'Give us a wave, Charlie,' yelled camera-toting Dubliners time after time, and Charlie invariably obliged. Dubliners call him the Teflon Chameleon, with his much admired ability· to change colour politically without anything sticking; and, given each country gets the political leadership it deserves, Charlie Haughey personifies the Irish trait of holding contradictory notions without any sign of strain.

'Is this one of the better St Patrick's Day parades?' I asked him, taking advantage of his accessibility as another American marching band did back-flips while playing 'Danny Boy' in front of him.

'It's not one a the worst,' came the politician's reply. And in fact, the general consensus was it had been one of the best.

In spite of the crowds, there was none of the clenched paranoia I was used to in London, and the unseasonably warm weather gave Grafton Street a southern European feel. From Trinity College to St Stephen's Green it was a mass of strolling, gossiping people, stopping at every opportunity to comment on any passing distraction.

And there were quite a few, from the street musicians and American Holy Rollers to local eccentrics and Dublin's very own punk fraternity – defiantly unchanged in appearance from its UK origins fourteen years earlier. I felt a distinct pang of nostalgia as an anorexic youth with acne and a nose ring led his shaven-headed girl-friend by on a dog lead. Ah, young love. Two young girls all in black and with

Dublin's punk fraternity is outmanoeuvred

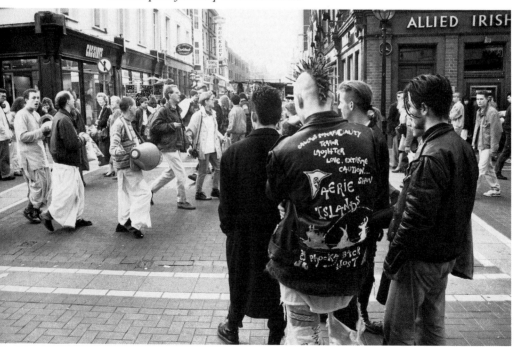

death's-head makeup ruined the effect by breaking into a Kylie Minogue song, while three surly youths in leather jackets posed impressively outside Bewley's café – until several nuns intent on lunch elbowed them effortlessly aside. In fact the entire punk fraternity had been outmanoeuvred that particular day by most of Dublin. Many Dubliners had gone in for a green rinse, and most had several pints of stout inside them and were determined to tap dance out of the constraints and conventions of church and state, at least for a few hours. Faced with this, the punks retreated en masse to the park, dyed their hair any colour other than green, and glumly sat in self-support groups downing large bottles of cider. I suppose it is not easy to be a rebel without a cause when you are surrounded by an entire town full of them all busily kicking over the traces.

As the Streets of Dublin race got under way and hundreds of joggers thundered around each corner, I took refuge in the Gresham hotel, which seemed to be having an indoor street party. Around me swirled the legendary crack of Dubliners which owes nothing to Colombian drug barons and a great deal to one of the last oral traditions in western Europe. Here words transcend mere communication in order to wrestle and pummel reality into submission, and leave the prosaic business of everyday life far behind – aided by several pints of Guinness, of course. And several hours and pints of stout later I too was in an excessively good mood tinging on the unreal, as I wended my way through the still Bacchanalian streets to the camper.

'Well,' I said to my two companions, 'what kind of day did you guys have, hey?'

Nothing. I tried again.

'Ah to be in Ireland, now that spring is here.'

Nada. What do cats know about fertility rites anyway?

2

The Ghosts of Molly Malone

'Look on the bright side, kid. Come the warm weather and I'll teach you to swim.' We were parked by the small, picturesque and smelly harbour of Bray, just down the coast from Dublin, and the Incorrigibles were very very bored. The exhilaration of seeing several thousand sea birds at the same time had quickly worn off when it dawned that most were bigger than they were, travelled in groups and had no qualms about attacking small mammals with Kamikaze inclinations. Even Cheesy admitted defeat when an outraged seagull the size of a small glider looked on in disbelief as she stalked it, then casually rose into the air at the crucial moment and shat on her head while giving a mocking cry that added insult to injury. Hence the promise of things to come. Besides, after several days of sharing space with a cat that on a scale of one to ten measured minus nine, the thought of an aquatic feline, preferably submerged, had great appeal. If nothing else, it might do something about the appalling smell that hovered about Cheesy like a small gas cloud around a very dim star. Perhaps she simply absorbed the stink of the polluted mud in the harbour. More likely it was due to the most haphazard method of washing this side of Old Mother Riley. If her personal hygiene left a little to be desired, her temperament left a great deal more. I know nothing about feline psychology, but I would have to assume Cheesy was not only emotionally deprived as a kitten, but the product of a broken home, domestic violence, inadequate parenting, poor diet, insufficient exercise, a poor learning environment and just about anything else that is likely to turn an innocuous young animal into a small psychopath with homicidal tendencies. Having shared space with her for a few days, I am now convinced that the relaxed, laid-back temperament of Pugwash is in fact a finely honed survival mechanism, geared to cope with a wildly contradictory mother who

An (understandably) cautious breakfast in Bray

purrs when she bites you and growls when stroked.

Whatever, having established the camper as their territorial base, they have both thrown feline caution to the winds that frequently blast over the harbour wall. If their days were spent sunbathing and studiously ignoring the whirling seabirds, the nights were given over to prowling the environs of the harbour with a nihilistic glee that would put a Class War warrior to shame. Which was fine by me, except that recently the temperature had nose-dived and brought with it one of the few things my two comedians really fear: cold feet. As I lay deep under the duvet listening to the wind thundering the surf against the outer walls of the harbour, the approaching patter of tiny feet made me wonder, not for the first time, if the local Mothercare shop sold very small bedsocks.

By day I explored Dublin while the nihilists slept off the previous night's excesses. The Dart commuter trains up to town were strangely unfamiliar after years of London commuting. Mainly because they run on time, are frequent and actually have enough seating. They follow the coastline, with panoramic views of Dublin Bay and place names that carry the resonance of Irish literature: from Bray to Dublin, Joyce to O'Brien.

They also carry a variety of characters that would do credit to either writer. After a few journeys, I began to give names to the more familiar faces. Pucknose had a pair of ears that might come in useful for picking up Sky television in areas of poor reception, a jaw that would be invaluable for cracking nuts at Christmas and a once prominent nose that now spread extravagantly across his face like – well, like a large hockey puck. Having made the mistake of responding to his engaging lopsided grin, I soon began to understand why his nose wandered across his face. The man had the kind of hobnailed sensibility that would cause Mother Theresa to commit murder. His opening gambit made me wonder if I needed to adjust the first letter of his nickname. The rest of the conversation confirmed that I did. As I gazed through my reflection in the window at the dusk turning the shallow water of the bay into a vast bowl of silver he piped up: 'Are you just admiring yourself there, or trying to take your mind off yourself with the view?'

The other passengers, all locals and clearly familiar with Pucknose's verbal gymnastics, leaned forward as one while keeping their eyes firmly on assorted reading material.

'. . . What?'

'Deaf too, eh? When He was handing out the necessaries, you must a bin well down the back.'

'Sorry?'

'It's not me you should be apologizing to, son. A good start would be your mother and father.' And so on. It was of course my first intro-duction to the crack of Dublin and Pucknose was an ace exponent. If the Irish are deeply tribal, then the apotheosis of that tribalism is Dublin, not so much a place as a race memory of Irishness enthusi-astically kept alive by a natural gregariousness, a delight in gossip, an eagle eye for the idiosyncratic, and those eight hundred pubs. And the crack is the glue that holds the entire edifice of myth, fantasy, tall tales and wishful thinking together. Conversations inevitably centre on Dublin and Dubliners, and whatever else is happening in the world, from Lithuania to Kuwait, has to percolate through the monomania. Given that, conversation is a lateral affair, jumping from one unrelated topic to another with varying and self-conscious skill. Which is why I suppose those legendary pubs and some railway carriages tend to be stocked with guys juggling their (conversational) balls. And not just indoors either. Temporarily disorientated by the newness of my surroundings and standing beside a big, heavy-looking church, I asked a passing local where St Patrick's Cathedral was.

'Across the road there,' he replied amiably. 'And if it's a miracle cure you're after for that eyesight, St Patrick's yeh man.' I wondered if he was related to Big Ears.

Dublin wit, like the exported variety in Liverpool, is both sharp and sentimental and rooted in precise observation. But it betrays a certain conservatism, particularly when confronted with the shock of the new. When feelings ran a little high on the fiftieth anniversary of the Easter rising, Nelson's column on O'Connell Street was blown up with an easy expertise that left the surrounding area unscathed. Unfortunately, when the Irish army blew up the remaining plinth, they wrought havoc for several blocks around. The crater left by the army is now occupied by a bronze nude reclining tastefully in flowing water. Inspired by James Joyce's Anna Livia, it personifies the Liffey. Dubliners instantly christened it the Floozy in the Jacuzzi. Another recent monument to Wolfe Tone set against large slabs of stone on St Stephen's Green is inevitably known as Tonehenge.

Perhaps the most striking feature of Dublin is not the few surviving Georgian squares or its legendary pubs, but the age of its inhabitants. Ireland has the youngest population in Europe and half the people of Dublin are under twenty-five. And it shows. Shoals of schoolchildren drift by, infest the shopping malls, and congregate on every street corner. Teenagers turn Henry Street and Grafton Street and the Templegate area into impromptu street parties. The exuberance of Dublin owes a lot to their vitality and free flow energy. The favourite fashion colour is still black, and youthful crowds, like flocks of starlings, swoop down to chatter around the slightest distraction before swirling on to the next street musician, entertainer,

Grafton Street musicians provide a distraction . . .

born-again enthusiast, pavement artist, or mere eccentric. There was a wide selection. As an inevitable group of Hare Krishna devotees crocodiled through a crowd of good-natured punks, I stopped to watch a street artist making a very good drawing of what looked like a scene from Dante's Inferno in modern dress. I should have known. Like Flaubert, I tend to attract animals and mad people.

'Do you recognize it?' asked the artist, with an odd American accent, as two of his cronies moved in on either side.

'Dante?' I hedged.

'Dublin.'

His entourage echoed doomily, 'Dublin.'

'Ah, right. That cloud above the chasm –'

'Grafton Street.'

as Young Dublin takes to the streets

'Right. That black cloud with all the screaming heads in it. It reminds me of Francis Bacon.' I was still under the impression I was talking to a street artist.

'Sin.'

The echo was repeated. 'Sin.'

A warning bell rang, but I soldiered on. 'And the cloud above it, with all the bright light shining out of it?'

'Redemption.'

'Redemption,' crooned the Greek chorus.

The penny finally dropped, and so had I, apparently, right in the middle of a group of Born Agains. It was a good five minutes before I extricated myself from them, during which time it was pointed out that I was riddled with sin, had nothing to look forward to except eternal damnation, but that a slim thread was dangling before me at this very moment that would lift me clear of life's temptations. All I had to do was sign on the dotted line, join the White Brotherhood of Jesus, and I was on my way. I demurred, reminded perhaps of the junk mail I regularly received back home which excitedly informed me that I had won several wonderful prizes, and all I had to do was call in and collect them from the nice Time Share people. We parted amiably, with the Brotherhood promising to pray for my immortal soul, and me promising (myself) to get my act together streetwise.

Over in Bewley's café, which was becoming a favourite of mine during the cold weather, I was reminded that I was still on a learning curve as far as Ireland was concerned. Now incorporated into Dublin's mythology, the vast high-ceilinged rooms, lined with the fine stained glass windows of Harry Clarke and centred on several large open fires, are still focal points for gossip, and the ghosts of Joyce, Behan and O'Brien – then on the wagon, presumably – still hover. Popular with students from nearby Trinity College, the café's buzz of conversation underlined the point that despite its size, Dublin still has the ambience of a country town. A group of students settled at my table and immediately engaged me in a long conversation about life in Dublin as seen through their perhaps rather privileged eyes. The first surprise was that they were all Catholics. The dire threat of excommunication for any Catholic attending this bastion of Protestant ethics was lifted in the early seventies, and now over seventy per cent of the students are of the faith. None of them came from Dublin, all of them intended to leave Ireland after graduation. In that respect at least they were typical of young people in Dublin today. It is still a staging post in the eternal search of the Irish for work.

As the students were all women, sexual politics loomed large in the conversation. Had the Irish male seen the light yet? Loud laughter.

'Absolutely not,' said Breda, a lively philosophy graduate with a cascade of the astonishing red hair that only seems to flourish in Ireland.

Was it a problem?

'It is for them. Personally I prefer the entirely unreconstructed ones. At least you know where you are with the buggers.' The others nodded wisely.

'It's the ones who come on strong about being your friend you have to watch,' said Clare, Celtic dark and reading sociology. Listening to them, I was transported back to my own years in higher education when, as a course tutor, I spent many an entertaining hour listening to the preoccupations of the students: sex, love, money, and even, occasionally, course subject problems. The world may have moved on, but student life, with one major difference (jobs), seemed much the same. In an arena where peer group pressure was paramount and home an occasional safe house in which to recuperate from the fray, these women at least seemed to be holding their own. But they still soaked up prevailing attitudes like sponges. All of them expected to marry and have children, although they all expected to go on working and build careers. I wished them luck anyway. Dublin is a good place to be young and optimistic.

Later, I met another side of Dublin. Across on the north side, it was advisable to take some basic precautions, especially around the shabby side streets off O'Connell Street on a late evening. With such an influx of young people, as in any large city, there were bound to be casualties. Dreams could soon dwindle into disillusionment on the hard stones of the street, and Dublin was invaded in the early eighties by dealers looking for new markets. As a result, the city now has a heavy drugs problem, and local smack heads are not averse to a little action to support their habit. On one of the 'quays' that line the Liffey, Sean spelled out the realities of being on the needle and HIV positive in a conservative Catholic country.

'It's like we're already dead, man. No one wants t' know, we don't exist. Even the doctors a terrified of us.' His voice droned on in that emotionless, blurred way that heroin addicts always seem to acquire, telling me his stories from the war zone of a life that at twenty-two was already in the shadows.

'Are you from Dublin originally?'

'The west coast, Kerry.'

'I'll be heading that way for the summer.'

For the first time, his seamed face became animated. 'Ah, it's a different world there . . . a different world.' He trailed off, as though someone had thrown a switch in him. I tried again.

'I hear it's very beautiful . . . couldn't you go home?' But he was gone now, lost inside himself somewhere. Maybe, in his own way, he was already home. We shook hands and I wished him luck, unable to find words that would not sound as empty as his own. He drifted away into the night like a ghost, to join the other wraiths in the nearby needle park, marginalized into oblivion.

By day the north side generally and Henry Street in particular seethes with young people intent on another local activity. Dubliners must be the most enthusiastic shoppers in Europe. Or they would be if they had the money. But with widespread unemployment and thirty per cent of them below the poverty line, a lot don't. So window shopping has become almost an art form – and yet another excuse and venue for gossip. Other cities have the constant drone of traffic as a background; Dublin has the human voice. The descendants of Molly Malone are more like the descendants of the Molly Maguires as they wheel their battered prams off O'Connell Street, selling anything from cheap paste jewellery to bananas.

One step up, the all-woman market in Moore Street thrives on a lethal mix of banter and bargaining. You take them on at your peril.

'Is this meat fresh?' asked one brave soul.

'If it was any fresher, luv, it'd be shiteing all over the pavement.'

At the ends of streets, men and boys stand for hours with sign-boards, and along the way children and women and men with faces ruined by drink sometimes beg, although nothing on the scale of London.

This Dickensian vitality on the street belies the far-reaching changes that Dublin has gone through in the last thirty years. Arriving in Dublin in 1960, a visitor would have seen a city little changed architecturally since the eighteenth century. Around that time a perceptive architectural critic wrote: 'The only reason why Dublin remained for so long the beautiful eighteenth-century city the English built is that the Irish were too poor to pull it down.' Not any more. Since then developers and speculators and simple human greed have turned Dublin into a pig's breakfast of architecture. Almost everywhere remnants of a Georgian heyday compete uneasily with sixties brutalism and occasional bizarre attempts to match the two. The demolitions

Molly Malone rides again

inspire as much local comment as the surviving buildings, and have found a place in the only thing that truly remains untouched by time: Dublin's mythology in a city half real and half remembered. As the money came flowing in during the sixties, a new breed of politicians emerged; one that combined post-nationalist nostalgia with a pragmatism and ruthless business skills that would have served them well in the Britain of the eighties. Prominent among them was a certain Charles J. Haughey who proclaimed: 'I, for one, have never believed that all architectural taste and building excellence ceased automatically with the passing of the eighteenth century.'

True to his word, Haughey sold the land he owned in the north of the city for a modern housing estate – and promptly used the hefty £150,000 profit to purchase a house designed by the great eighteenth-century architect Gandon. With the politicians clearing the way and providing the incentives through an insatiable need for more space for a growing army of government officials, Dublin's business community must have thought Christmas had come early for much of the sixties and seventies, recalling James Joyce's words about those who would not only sell their country for fourpence, but get down on their bended knees to thank the Almighty Christ they had a country to sell. As the centre's population was decanted into the purgatory of outlying estates that seemed to be deliberately designed to undermine their natural gregariousness, the fabric was torn down and replaced by something more functional or, when the money finally ran out, simply left to rot.

Those Dubliners who did protest were given a sharp lesson in post-nationalist politics along the lines of: Did not the English build Georgian Dublin on the backs of the Irish? Despite the obvious cynicism of this appeal to grassroots nationalism, it touched a nerve among indigenous Dubliners. Mainly because the myth of the Easter Rising – where a namesake of my mother's family, James Connolly, led the Citizens' Army – was just that as far as Dubliners were concerned. The city never had played a central role in the history of Irish Nationalism and 1916 was no exception. Most Dubliners either ignored the Rising, argued against it or took part enthusiastically in an epic spree of looting while carefully avoiding the shooting. Not until the British began executing the leaders did attitudes change, and the potency of the Easter Rising that has fuelled Irish Nationalism ever since owes not a little to Dublin's guilty conscience and an uncontrollable impulse to hog the limelight. Their tendency to be more Irish than the Irish and self-appointed guardians at the cutting edge of all things Irish has probably provided a useful defence against the criticisms of more devout Nationalists: that the cosmopolitan port city of Dublin is in the same league as the great whore of Babylon; ever open to offers from a wicked world. Whatever, faced with the prospect of being ravished, Dubliners remained true to their instincts, lay back and thought of Ireland.

If Dublin is full of the ghosts of past architecture, underneath all that endless talk, the wit and banter, is perhaps a sadness at something else lost and changed and gone forever, rooted in the internal exile of the new estates and the diasporas that have created an Ireland abroad.

As that ultimate Dubliner and poet of its streets, Flann O'Brien, once wrote: 'We filled up the loneliness of our two souls with the sounds of our two voices.'

Back by the harbour in Bray, two other souls had been filling up their loneliness. Unbeknown to me, the Incorrigibles had gone walkies and met a small dog on the quay. A very expensive small dog with an owner of some power and influence in the town. The inevitable had occurred, a perforated dog had disappeared over the horizon and an enraged owner had tracked the perforators back to the camper. Which is why, early the next morning, I had a little chat with two men in uniforms, who kindly gave me directions for leaving Bray harbour: basically, any direction. The Garda were unfailingly polite, as people often are when they carry guns. As we drove off into the dawn, heading (appropriately, I suppose) for the once legendary bandit country of the Wicklow mountains, I had a little heart-to-heart with my own two bandits on the need to respect the customs of a host country. For example, dogs chased cats, and not the other way round. Judging by the self-satisfied smirks in the passenger seat, I too was filling up the loneliness of the void with the sound of my own voice.

3

Sex and the Single Priest

Life had settled down to a kind of routine which I hoped I had imposed on the Incorrigibles and I knew they had imposed on me. The situation underlined one of the fundamental laws of any relationship between people and cats. Cats train people.

Pugwash, for instance, languished along the curve of the dashboard, muffling the speakers and vibrating to the sounds of Van Morrison and Puccini. Having tried everything from Public Enemy rap to Guns 'n' Roses heavy metal at full volume to shift him, I was resigned to spending the driving hours listening to the music through several inches of comatose cat.

Cheesy, on the other hand, still thrilled with the novelty of it all, perched on the back of the driving seat like a parrot and anchored herself to the back of my head whenever we hit a steep bit which, given we were exploring the Wicklow mountains, occurred frequently.

Things could have been worse, of course, and with Cheesy they often were. Either the excitement of travel or something in the local water had had a disastrous effect on her digestive system. Every few minutes a sound like a slowly deflating balloon had me reaching for the handle to wind down the window before the fumes steamed up my glasses. Not content with being Ireland's most flatulent cat, she kept up a constant chatter from growls to mews and a particularly irritating whirruping sound. What with the music muff on the one hand and a flatulent parrot come garrulous granny on the other, life in the camper got a little tense at times. Which is why a Ford Transit could sometimes be seen with two cats peering huffily from the purdah of the rear window. What the few motorists in those parts thought of a passing vehicle with two life-like nodding cats in the back remains unrecorded.

What the Irish think of their own domesticated animals is recorded in the many pet cemeteries scattered throughout the land and particularly in the grounds of the great houses. Sex, death, land and religion are the keys to understanding the Irish, more than one home-grown writer has said (usually when safely out of the country), so Powerscourt House, near Enniskerry, seemed a reasonable start to self-improvement. Along with Ireland's highest waterfall nearby, it has some of the finest landscaped gardens in the country, with the Sugarloaf mountain standing alone as a perfectly shaped back-drop.

Given it also has the largest private pet cemetery in Ireland, it seemed like a good idea (at the time) to take my two comedians walkabout. Perhaps intimations of their mortality might give me the edge in the power struggle in the van. And then again, perhaps not.

The tourist season had yet to get under way, and the grounds were deserted. The burnt-out shell of the big house from a fire in 1974 – Ireland's great houses have a remarkable tendency to go up in smoke – had a Hammer Horror look about it, particularly when the mournful cry of peacocks drifted down from the woods. To add to the atmosphere, the ruin was infested with small black dogs, the yapping of which reached a climax as my two deviants strolled by with the feigned innocence of Class War anarchists passing a burned-out Porsche. 'All right, don't overdo it,' I muttered as they stopped to wash elaborately under the gaze of the tiny dogs two storeys safely above them.

Reaching the cemetery took forever – you do not take cats for a walk, they take you – as they explored every single bush and tree along the way. Caution, however, did not extend to stalking a large male peacock in the Japanese garden which, after staring at them in macho disbelief, flounced into a display that stunned even them into a tactical retreat. After I extracted Cheesy yet again from a rabbit hole – her whiskers clearly fall short of her middle-age spread – we finally arrived at the cemetery. Whatever the significance of the place for the residents, the expanse of light sandy soil meant only one thing to my two unbelievers. As I perused the headstones – 'Little Bots – the dearest friend', 'Sting – faithful beyond human fidelity' – my own dearest pair, unfaithful beyond human infidelity, enthusiastically dug little holes before plonking themselves down to meditate on the meaning of peacocks.

The cemetery contained any number of dogs, ponies, horses, and even cows, but significantly no cats. Given the name of the latest addition to the ever fertile royal family, I was intrigued to see that, as the mother of seventeen calves, one cow was called Eugenie. Synchronicity is never far away in Ireland.

Neither are park wardens, apparently. As I inspected more headstones that read like a page in the *Guardian* on Valentine's Day – Modger, Doodle, Taffy Topaz, Busky Chow Chow, The Wup – a large, bald and clearly enraged warden with a head like a boiled potato and a mouth like a slit in a carrot bore down on us, and my contemplation of the sentimentality of the Irish came to an abrupt end. As we left rather more rapidly than we had arrived, I pointed out that the regulations said nothing about cats, only dogs.

'Well, they will from now on,' he hissed ominously.

'Well done, guys,' I said, as we headed across the bleak peat bogs

Pugwash has intimations of mortality . . .

of the Wicklow mountains for Glendalough and one of the origins of Irish sexuality. 'You just made it into Irish law.' The Muff and the Parrot were unimpressed.

Glendalough, the valley of two lakes, is in the heart of the Wicklow mountains, and on a warm late spring evening, the solitude and peace of the place still refreshes those parts which inner city life usually neglects. Little wonder it attracted a certain Kevin, back in the sixth century. He soon became so successful as a hermit that he attracted pilgrims from far and wide, each of them seeking peace and solitude. So strong was this desire that by the tenth century Glendalough had become a monastic city famous throughout Ireland and crowded with monks, all presumably trying to ignore each other while they communed with nature and an elusive God.

Kevin himself, later St Kevin, was, like many saints, made of stern stuff. A man of high birth and attractive with it – the name in Gaelic

Cheesy does not

means 'well featured' – he loved animals but, again like so many saints, was not so keen on women. Hence his departure to Glendalough. On arrival, it is said he stood in the water of the loch with arms upraised for so long that birds nested on him. When a persistent admirer called Kathleen tracked him down to his isolated cave, known still as Kevin's Bed, he attacked her with a bunch of nettles and threw her into the loch. Not surprisingly, she promptly became a nun. It is unlikely St Kevin's contemporaries ever referred to him as Kev.

At a time when the most effective form of birth control for women was to point and giggle (it probably still is), Kevin's sexual politics were par for the course, and celibacy a convenient response to both personal sexual angst and the power games of early Christianity, concerned as it then still was to eliminate the last vestiges of matricentral

Opposite: Pugwash contemplates Ireland's highest waterfall . . .

Cheesy does not

influence. It is appropriate that this period of Christianity is com-memorated by the round towers and that Glendalough has one of the best examples in Ireland: a massive 140ft all-purpose granite phallus with unreachable windows that still thrusts perkily into the sky above the ruins of a city once populated by hundreds of celibates. By the nineteenth century, Glendalough had become so notorious a place for bargain basement pilgrims – seven visits equalled one visit to Rome towards a papal indulgence – that several hundred special constables were sometimes required to pacify the drunken brawlers who had come to pay homage to Kevin's vision of peace and tranquillity.

Celibacy today is as prominent in Irish religious affairs as those round towers are in the Irish landscape, and consequently plays an important part in the domestic affairs of Ireland. Indeed, as one ex-priest explained to me, it is one of the most important issues facing the Catholic Church today and has led to a serious crisis in recruitment to the priesthood. Meeting him, I might have expected to find a gaunt, angst-ridden paranoiac man living in the shadows. What I found was a small, chubby, genial and gentle man, devoted to his wife and children and still taking an active interest in community and church affairs.

'One argument is that priests have a choice in the matter, when the fact is many do not,' he said. 'I began my vocational training at nine, and not until I was in my late twenties did I seriously question my vow of celibacy. How could I? I'd never known anything else. And as the sexual attitudes changed, not only my own personal needs, but the personal needs of the people I tended to, women especially, came into conflict with the teachings of the Church. And so I found myself in conflict as I struggled to deal with a society that was changing while teaching that nothing must change.' After a long and difficult struggle, he left the Church. Had he regretted it? 'I shall always regret it,' he said. 'But I shall always feel it was the right decision. I was taught to believe that celibacy enhanced me, and I learned that in fact it diminished me. I think that coming to terms with my sexuality liberated many other things in me, and now I think I'm more whole than I ever was before.'

It was hardly surprising he felt liberated after so many years of com-pulsory celibacy – he was consistent in his argument that voluntary celibacy was a matter for the individual – but I wondered if he took a rosier view than I could now of the changes in sexual attitudes over the last twenty-five years. Being a member of a generation that came of age in the sixties, I have a growing number of friends, particularly women, who view the sexual revolution with mixed feelings.

'I thought I was free to say yes,' said one recently. 'Looking back, it seems I was forever finding myself in a position of being unable to say no. I'm beginning to wonder who liberated who?' Another, a single parent, has decidedly mixed feelings about divorce after years of struggling to raise her children, worrying about the long-term emotional consequences for them, and fending off predatory males while trying to find a personal life for herself. Given feminist rhetoric has made even less of an impact on Irish society over the years, I wondered if the abandonment of the vow of celibacy would make much difference to the realities of sexual politics in Ireland.

'It would,' the ex-priest said, 'because the Church plays such an intimate part in people's lives here. The issues of divorce, abortion, and contraception are all basically affected by the Church's perception of those issues. So abortion is still illegal, the only country in Europe now, divorce is virtually impossible, and contraception still frowned upon. That's the simple measure of the difference: the difference of having a choice or not.

'What you and your friends are dealing with are the responsibilities that follow from the freedom of choice. But we have to deal with the absence of choice and the consequences that follow from that. A situation where nineteen thousand couples in Dublin alone live in the nether land of legal separation. Where several thousand Irish women last year went abroad for abortions, and returned to live with the trauma, often alone and without support. This is a country with the youngest population in Europe because of the birth rate, and where so many of our young people, who are always the future, must emigrate still to find work. Yes, I do think the vow of celibacy amongst the clergy makes a difference, because it makes the Church more fearful of allowing the people to make their own choices in these matters.'

We talked then and for a long time about the roller-coaster of male sexuality, with its highs and sudden lows, its traps and contradictions, the daft generalizations about it that ignore the existence of free will but still manage to wound, and all its conflicting needs and fears and anxieties that can sabotage even the most rewarding of relationships. Which led us inevitably on to the difference between being in love and loving someone. Clearly we had a rather different perspective, perhaps because our experiences had been different – to say the least. The ex-priest waxed lyrical about how falling in love was akin to the ecstatic experience of saints, while loving someone was similar to prayer and meditation. While allowing that loving someone sometimes required the patience and qualities of a saint, falling in love in my experience was rather like having 'flu on speed, with judgment and common sense early casualties, and the libido acquiring a life all of its own: 'It's like being on heat,' groaned a suffering friend recently.

Despite the different paths taken over the last twenty years, we had it seemed reached similar conclusions about our own sexuality. And although we were still prisoners of gender, held fast in our own absurd little round towers, at least we had climbed far enough to glimpse another landscape beyond the ruins of a world still run by Kevins. Did he think men and women could ever be truly themselves with each other?

'I do,' he beamed, 'I really do,' his enthusiasm like a warm fire as I drove off into the chill of the evening.

Back in the van, not a lot had changed. As the muffled voice of Pavarotti filtered through Pugwash, Cheesy resumed her mad parrot routine. In an attempt to stem the chatter, I reviewed a question with her.

'Do you think men and women can ever be themselves with each other, kid?'

I should have known. A familiar sound like a slowly deflating balloon added one more small cat-shaped hole to the ozone layer over Ireland. As I wound down the window yet again, I was reminded of another basic trait all cats share.

They are incorrigible cynics.

4

Love and Death and the Cycling Connection

The weather in Ireland is, I was reliably informed before I left home, unreliable. This is true. Having left an east coast still occasionally blitzed by wintry showers, I arrived in county Kerry on the west coast loaded down with wellies, oilskins and thick woollies to find I was in the middle of the driest spring for thirty years while a brazen sun blazed down from an azure sky. Which was why I found myself suddenly pottering about in a pair of shorts and with a bad case of sunburn. Not so the Incorrigibles. Ever adaptable and part Persian among several other varieties, they were busily moulting at a rate that would have them entirely bald by high summer. Given the attention they already received, that was about all I needed.

'If you two think I'm shelling out for a pair of custom-made posing pouches to cover up the rude bits, think again,' I said, as yet another blizzard of fur swept through the van.

I had settled on the Iveragh peninsula for a while near Kenmare, on a camp site with panoramic views of a dramatic landscape. And cats on a camp site, I discovered, had the same impact on people as a herd of elephants down the Strand. They recognized the species, but wondered what the hell they were doing there. So did I, actually.

Pugwash, invariably hands-on and user-friendly, took it all in his stride. For Cheesy, however, this new-found attention came as a stunning surprise. Conditioned to having the same effect on people as Freddy in *Nightmare on Elm Street*, she wore the kind of bemused expression you might possibly find on Saddam Hussein's face at a Bar Mitzvah. For some reason, the mainly German tourists in the area found her atrocious temper and unnerving mood swings deeply endearing, which could be worrying for the future of German reunification, and did nothing for the management structure in our camper. My entire power base, centred upon the can-opener, was severely

The Incorrigibles engage in a mutual grooming session

Opposite: confronted by an ascendency of goats

undermined by frequent gifts of choice pieces of wild salmon and brown trout – the area has some excellent fishing – which were reverently laid outside the camper every evening by besotted Aryans. The moulting twosome subsequently took to parading around the camp site with all the abject humility of Storm-troopers on Kristallnacht, although they occasionally got their comeuppance. As when two young goats invaded the van . . .

Never having seen goats before, Cheesy probably assumed they were a peculiar breed of dog, and a lifetime of tactical surprise – dogs rarely expect cats to run towards them – had given her an unrealistic perception of her combat potential. Which presumably explained why one enraged cat flew into the camper – and promptly flew out again, tossed by a young, puzzled goat. Undeterred, she launched herself at the enemy again, and once again shot into space, furious and bewildered. As a small circle of admirers gathered, I collected up the bundle of spitting fury and removed her from the combat zone.

'Your pussy cat is very brave,' said a woman in a Day-glo track suit.

'My pussy cat is a complete dickhead,' I muttered to the Kamikaze

one, who had turned her frustration on me and was trying to remove a hand. 'Call it a learning experience,' I added, as I locked her in the television room to cool off. Revenge was later extracted from the local small mammal population (again) and the next morning the area under the van looked as if Pol Pot had been a night visitor.

Coming from one of the world's largest conurbations, where silence is anything under eighty decibels, I found the Irish countryside peaceful almost beyond belief, although far from quiet, particularly at this time of year, when all the feathered couples in the area are operating a protect and survive policy. Ornithologists claim that bird song often translates into the kind of friendly banter you find down the Old Kent Road around closing time on a Friday night. 'One hop closer, yeh worm-gobbling tit, an' you'll get this beak across yeh. An' take them beady eyes off me bird an' all.' That sort of thing. Of course, something gets lost in translation, science having the depressing tendency to rationalize perceived phenomena in the light of our own species' experience. Not that our own species is entirely immune to the spring surge.

Camp sites have an endearing camaraderie that is usually absent from hotels. Among other things, they are about sharing territory and experiences while hotels are about exclusivity and (hopefully) private experiences. Which is why the earth is more likely to move if you invite the partner of your dreams to a three-star hotel rather than a three-star camp site for that dirty weekend. Not everybody, though, is deterred by lumpy ground and the thin walls of a tent, as a nearby German couple vociferously proved for three nights running. They arrived wearing leather shorts and riding a tandem, so I should have known. In another nearby tent, two Australian women kept up a running commentary on the evening's performance and the unreliability of the male libido, as only Australian women can.

'What's worse than a tumescent male, Shirley?'

'A detumescent one, har har har.'

None of this put the heroic German couple off their stride. It was probably all that practice on the tandem. As the rhythmic moans reached yet another climax, the Australians gave a round of applause, along with a cry of, 'Go for gold, sport!'

★　　★　　★

Elsewhere, things were a little different in this heartland of traditional Ireland, as the story of the Kerry babies graphically illustrated. A young unmarried mother called Joanne Hayes gave birth to a son who died almost immediately of natural causes and whose body she concealed in a ditch on her family farm. At the same time, another dead baby, also a boy, was washed ashore on a remote beach in the same county of Kerry forty-three miles away. This baby's body had twenty-eight stab wounds and a broken neck. Two weeks later the young woman was charged with the murder of the second infant, even though her own child was found and forensic evidence from blood typing showed that the second baby could not be hers. The Garda argued that she had borne twins, conceived by different fathers within a twenty-four-hour period, and reasoned that this was likely since she already had a child by her lover and was therefore an immoral woman.

In the subsequent tribunal of inquiry into police methods, the young woman was subjected to five days of cross-examination about her moral standards and 'physical appetites'. This was only five years ago and local people still argue the pros and cons of the case.

If the social mores of the area are as convoluted as the landscape, the weather was as unpredictable as the prevailing moral climate, and yielded equally strange results. Spring and summer vegetation appeared together, and the results were spectacular. Catkins still hung on the trees while great swathes of bluebells created an hallucination of lavender in every wood and primroses lined the banks of half empty streams. Foxgloves were already blooming among hedgerows ablaze with fuchsia, and even the yellow bog iris had started to appear. Across the bare hillsides, long denuded of trees, the flowering gorse was scattered like small explosions. The heat and close proximity of the Gulf Stream, which allows the cultivation of palm trees, lent the area a sub-tropical feel, and everything gave off a warm fruity smell.

Walking through such a magnificent landscape so rich in vegetation, it was hard to realize that it had endured the worst of the terrible Irish famine of the 1840s. I was heading for the Black Valley, so called because its entire population was wiped out by starvation and disease at the height of the 'great hunger'. Atavistic memories of those times permeate the whole area. In Kenmare, the horror reached its peak in

1847, when the recently completed workhouse, inundated with the starving poor, became a charnel house as disease took its toll in the overcrowded buildings, which a medical officer's report written in the May of that year makes clear: '22.5.47: During these past two months, the number of those suffering from fever, dysentery and measles averaged 220 per week and 153 inmates died during the same period. The Workhouse is not only a great hospital for which it was never intended or adapted but an engine for producing disease and death.' Irish history here is forever the skull beneath the skin.

From Moll's Gap at the top of the pass between Killarney and Kenmare, the still mostly deserted valley stretched across to the foot of Ireland's highest mountains, Macgillycuddy's Reeks. The sandstone slopes and limestone valley floor, shaped and rounded by the last ice age, showed steel and umber in the heat haze. As in the Lake District, an illusion of huge mass and space is created here in a relatively small area, and the valley itself seemed vast – and empty. There was little vegetation and the silence was so profound that a bird's distant wings could be heard beating like a faint pulse. From the valley floor, the remains of long abandoned fields struggled up the higher mountain slopes. They were a last desperate attempt to cultivate every scrap of marginal land before the catastrophic failure of the potato crop overwhelmed the valley's population. Even now, on a perfect May day, the place gave off a sombre trace memory of past trauma and human misery. A line from Godot summed up their lives towards the end. 'They gave birth astride a grave.'

The Great Famine left a psychic scar on the Irish character that manifests itself in what even many Irish see as a morbid sentimentality about Ireland, and still provides ammunition for the Nationalists. Over a million people perished in just five years, three million more emigrated over the next twenty-five in the diaspora that created Ireland abroad, and the population was halved, never to recover. Even today this part of Ireland is one of the most sparsely inhabited in Europe.

And standing there, in that haunted valley on a perfect spring day, I suddenly remembered a more recent and even more terrible tragedy. Perhaps it was the oppressive silence, devoid of the sounds of any living thing, that triggered the memory, but I suddenly realized it was exactly a year to the day that I had stood by the punishment block in Auschwitz and felt a total despair over the depths of human nature and the enormity of the holocaust. On either side, stretching away to the distant, ominous haze of barbed wire, stood the rows of huts of the old Polish army barracks that had once contained unimaginable human misery and now housed pathetic remains, from mounds of human hair and spectacles to children's clothing.

As we left a tiny punishment cell, the inside of its thick wooden door scored by the frantic nails of suffocating prisoners, I asked my guide and survivor of the camp: 'Why in God's name did they have a punishment block in this place?'

'The administration lived in constant fear of an uprising,' she replied. 'Auschwitz was ruled by terror, and they always felt the need to remind us of it. Everything here had a part to play in that, everything that happened had a purpose. Auschwitz was an engine of death,' she added, echoing the medical officer in Kenmare on another May morning long before. 'Maybe the hardest thing to understand about the camp is that every part of it was designed to achieve its function. Nothing was ever left to chance in this place. Nothing.'

And a year later, I remembered that in Auschwitz too, on a beautiful May morning, no birds sang, no one spoke, there were just the silent accusations of a million ghosts, rising after a while on the edge of the mind to a whisper like leaves on an invisible wind.

Auschwitz was the ultimate lesson in what prejudice could lead to; and standing in that beautiful, silent valley and the consequences of another century's prejudice, a valley which had once been an unnecessary tomb for so many people, I began to have a clearer understanding of the Irish.

The only person I was to meet during the whole day in the valley was tall and abnormally thin and, despite the heat, wore one of those old-fashioned dark suits labourers still don when working out in the fields. It was probably my state of mind, but he looked like the grave digger in *Hamlet* as he cheerfully wielded a spade and dug peat out of a long coffin-like ditch, entirely alone and surrounded by huge open spaces.

'It's a grand day!' he yelled across from less than three feet away.

Like a moth to a flame, I was drawn by the voice of a man who turned out to be Ireland's Most Enthusiastic Turf Cutter.

For the next forty-five minutes, my eyes glazed over as I was given a crash course in digging peat that would last me to the end of my days. This man had dug peat all his life and I had a distinct feeling I was the one he had chosen to tell the uncensored story to. It was like being trapped in a lift with someone from Wandsworth into transactional analysis and obsessed with Marks and Spencer. Detail after tiny detail piled up like the turf itself, and I began to have fond memories of other bog people; the ones in the British Museum who had been dead for five thousand years. Even as I managed finally to get away, glassy-eyed and near deaf – he had the loudest voice I've ever heard – he followed me across half the field, still yelling about slanes and underfooting and clamping. I was beginning to see why he worked entirely alone with a lot of space around him. Later in the day I saw him approaching on one of those big old-fashioned sit-up-and-beg Raleigh bikes, and I hid in a ditch. As he sailed by, spindly legs whirling like pistons, he was still chuntering on about cutting turf. He probably still is.

It was almost dark when I got back to the camp site. I had been walking for eleven hours and long ago given up any attempt to climb Carrantuohill, at just over a modest thousand metres Ireland's highest mountain. The Irish have a tendency to interchange miles and kilometres and what I thought was twenty miles I later discovered was over thirty. As I tottered to the van and two overweight, balding cats, I met the German entrants for this year's sex olympics.

'Did you climb the mountain?' they asked.

'Well, actually, I sort of circumnavigated it.'

'We did not see you around the top.'

'You climbed the mountain? After cycling all that way?' I was lost in admiration, given the aerobics every night. What did these people eat?

'No, no, our friends the Australians gave us a lift.'

Friends? Maybe too much sex makes you deaf after all.

Black Valley, home of a million ghosts

Cheesy, en route to a posing pouch

That night as I lay in the van with my gently throbbing feet, the usual post-dinner snow-storm of fur whirled around me and fatigue led my mind to idly wander around my own particular Irish Question. Maybe if I put the little buggers in plastic bags with small holes for the heads and feet, then I could empty the bags just once a day. Cheesy and Pugwash finished grooming. Pugwash yawned, Cheesy added another hole to the ozone layer, and they both slipped out of the ever open window for another night of carnage. Maybe I should just put them both in black plastic bags, on bin day.

Outside, the last of the twilight revealed the blue mass of the distant Caha mountains, the edge of the peaks etched against the sky as delicately as a pencil line. L' Heure Bleue, a newly arrived French couple called it, and here in the far west of Ireland, with its bone-deep history and troubled memories, only a distant sound, strangely familiar and like a pair of bellows with a leak, intruded upon the stillness of a perfect evening. The Germans were going for gold.

5

Levitating Dogs, Inflammable Budgies, and Skellig's Synchronicity

All together now! Oh, I do like to be beside the seaside, I do like to be beside the sea . . . Nothing. Les Miserables continued to slump in the shade and stare out mournfully at the stunning seascape of Ballinskelligs Bay at the end of Western Europe. I suppose when you stand a mere eight inches at the shoulder, the vast spaces of the Iveragh peninsula, popularly known as the Ring of Kerry, can look a little daunting. For whatever reason, the dynamic duo had greeted beach life with all the enthusiasm of John Gummer at a Vegan convention. The initial reaction was cautious approval, if only because the miles of sandy beach provided endless prospects for digging those inevitable little holes. But then the tide came in, confusion reigned, and only intensified when it went out again. After several days you might think the penny would drop, but no. As the timeless ritual repeated itself, there they sat, two little black and white figures like negatives in a technicoloured world, still bemused by the entire proceedings.

Meanwhile the Irish continued to be fascinated by a pair of mobile cats and never a day went by without several lengthy conversations, usually on the merits of dogs versus cats as the ideal pets. I invariably came down on the side of dogs as my two preened in their new high profile life while keeping a sharp lookout for handouts.

The locals also seemed to have a rather ambivalent attitude towards their own pets, as I discovered while waiting at a little railway crossing with automatic gates. I got into conversation with a man who had a pair of ears that would put Prince Charles in the shade, and he was accompanied by a subdued, wild-looking sheepdog. As he casually looped the dog's lead over the end of the crossing's barrier, he commented affectionately on my two glaring out of the van at the dog.

'Now there's an unusual thing. Are they trained and everything?' he asked.

The Incorrigibles consider the eternal mystery of tides

'Oh yes, everything.'

Just then the train passed and suddenly the barrier shot up, taking the dog with it. As we gazed up at the animal suspended twenty feet above us, he said casually: 'Will you look at that stupid bloody dog? Not a grain a sense.' As the Incorrigibles looked on with unconcealed glee he asked: 'A cat's that stupid?'

'Absolutely,' I said loyally.

'Will yeh get down from there!' he bawled at the petrified dog.

'I think it might need a hand,' I suggested.

'Ah, there'll be another train along soon,' he said. 'Do you think there's anything in this mad cow business?'

I left him reading his newspaper and waiting for a train to come by while his airborne dog, still entangled in the metal skirt of the gate, gazed down in mute panic.

'All right,' I said as the gargoyles crowded gleefully to the back window for a last look at the levitated dog. Some cats have an evil sense of humour.

Before returning to the Iveragh peninsula we had spent several days exploring the hinterland of Killarney, a once pretty town that had been discovered by the Romantic movement in the nineteenth century and now thinks of itself as the centre of the Irish Lake District with all that is likely to entail. The surrounding countryside is still magnificent and unspoilt, but the town had that fake overpainted look of a place that sells itself daily to the highest bidder, which at this time of year meant mainly Americans enthusiastically searching for their roots (I could talk). Fortunately this ethnic Disneyland was the exception rather than the rule, and a few miles in any direction brought you back into the remarkable landscape of Kerry and, in our case, Mrs O'Connell's B and B farm. I felt the need to sleep in a real bed for a night, undisturbed by small enthusiastic nocturnal predators comparing notes at three in the morning.

Mrs O'Connell was delightfully friendly, and her immaculately conceived living room had a little shrine in one corner complete with a Day-glo photograph of the Pope, a small plastic figure of Christ that lit up in the dark, and a portrait of St Patrick with eyes that followed you around the room. My heart sank, though, when I saw the budgie cage. For some strange reason, things happen when budgies hover in my vicinity.

'Do your pussy cats like budgies?' asked Mrs O'Connell.

Does Michael Heseltine wear a hairnet in bed?

'Maybe they'd like the run a the farmyard,' said Mrs O'Connell wisely as Pugwash and Cheesy sat entranced below a nervously fluttering Tweety Pie.

As I sank into the leatherette settee, I suddenly had an attack of déjà vu. In another time on another settee, a budgie accounted for one of the darkest episodes of my adolescence . . . The love of my life had invited me round to meet her parents. Besotted by unrequited lust, I even wore a suit, the only one I ever owned, and teetered in on a pair of brand new Cuban-heeled boots. Seated by an open fire in the front room kept for best, and juggling tea and tinned salmon sandwiches, I strove to make a good impression. This included enthusing about the mother's budgie. Encouraged by my new-found admiration of fancy birds other than her daughter, she insisted on letting the sodding thing out. As it flew chirpily about the room, mother and daughter departed for refills and then – disaster. Uncrossing cramped legs just as the budgie flew by, I caught it with the toe of my boot and it cannoned into the depths of the coal fire where it disappeared in a puff of smoke. As I sat there, stunned, the mother of my soon-to-be-ex-girlfriend returned.

'Is Percy keeping you entertained?' she trilled.

'Oh yes,' I gasped before collapsing into giggles that all the anticipated lust in the world couldn't stem. I was of course deemed unsuitable. Not because of the budgie. Nobody ever did figure out where that went, and I was in no fit state to explain. It was those alarming fits of giggles. As I tottered to the door, the voice of doom pronounced the verdict behind me.

'Can't you do better than that? The lad's lift only goes up to the second floor.'

In Mrs O'Connell's living room, I eyed Tweety Pie nervously.

'I usually let it out for a little flutter this time on an evening,' she said.

'Really? Would you mind if I had an early night, Mrs O'Connell?'

The next day I went for a long cycle ride and left the cats to explore the wonders of farm life. It was a warm sunny day and I arrived back tired but refreshed by a combination of traffic-free roads and exhilarating landscape. Pugwash sauntered across for his customary stroke while what presumably was the farm cat, beautifully clean and fluffed out like a powder puff, minced by self-consciously across the far side of the farmyard.

'By the way,' said Mrs O'Connell over tea, 'we had to wash one a the cats.'

'Sorry?'

'It fell in the midden, so we had to shampoo it. She came up lovely and clean!' The powder puff mincing across the farmyard was – Cheesy? 'It took three on us and we had to wear hedging gloves. She kicked up a terrible fuss.'

I bet she did. As I drove back to Kenmare the next day, I just couldn't resist singing 'I'm going to wash that man right outa my hair' as Cheesy, fragrant for the first and last time in her life, glared out of the rear window. It's not often I have the edge on that cat.

Back on the Iveragh peninsula not a lot had changed, which was part of its charm, albeit an illusory one. The area had been invaded many times in its history by successive waves of people, each leaving its mark, from Bronze Age settlers to the 'blow-ins', as the locals called the hippies of the 1970s. This part of Ireland has always attracted a certain kind of wanderer who, coming up against the vastness of the Atlantic, decides that journey's end has finally been reached. We met two of the latest wanderers camped by Templenoe pier on the Kenmare river, complete with those inevitable New Age accessories, an old converted bus and a thin shaggy dog on a piece of string: Ben. Like his owners, Ben was a vegan with an easy-going nature that drastically reduced his chances for territorial superiority over two veterans from a South London battleground. For believers in reincarnation, Ben was probably a Buddhist monk in a previous existence, Pugwash a poet writing odes to nature with a homicidal subtext, and Cheesy a Leeds fan who expired on the terraces of Millwall in mid-riot. After a brief skirmish, Ben – a sadder and wiser dog – retreated to the nearby wood, from which he timidly emerged at meal times after the Incorrigibles had been locked in the van.

Ben's owners, Caroline and Neil, had left England in January and would be travelling until the autumn. Young and idealistic, they had chosen to opt out for a year to wander around the west of Ireland. I asked Caroline, an ex-teacher from a Steiner school, why?

'I just hated what the country has become. Everybody seemed so unhappy and driven, without seeming to know why, and the atmosphere was always so tense, it made you feel clenched up all the time. I don't know. I just felt that something's gone terribly wrong.'

Neil was less articulate and rather more dreamy, possibly because he was a spliff enthusiast, but also because he carried around a typical New Age ragbag of beliefs that ranged from concern over the rain forests to a surreal idea that all meat had within it the final agonies and fear of the abattoir, which then passed into the food chain. He spent several days in long conversations with Cheesy on the error of her ways. Judging by the body count each morning, old cloth-ears was unrepentant.

The two young travellers were both fairly typical of the rag, tag and ponytailed army of dissenters that has emerged over the eighties in Britain: running away from personal trauma or lack of opportunity, rejecting the selfish, inverted values of Thatcherism and

embracing an unfocused vision of a better world. And as they sit with their 'homeless and hungry' placards, squat in the places no one else wants, travel the country and occasionally run amok in Trafalgar Square, outraged Authority, forgetful of its own youth, uses a sledge-hammer of incomprehension to crack their youthful nuts. Even in the more tolerant climate of Ireland, the high profile bus and Mad Max 2 appearance had drawn the attention of the Garda, who regularly checked up on Ben's owners. It never was easy to be young, but it did seem to be getting harder.

As I drove away from Templenoe and a much relieved Ben, I wondered about all the other people who had travelled here and looked for some kind of respite from the everyday world with all its imperfections. The area has a long tradition for escapism and I was heading for the ultimate sanctuary: that Ultima Thule of the spirit, Skellig Michael.

The Great Skellig is a near barren rock eight miles out in the Atlantic and, along with Little Skellig and the Blasket Islands, it is the most westerly point in Europe. Landing is only possible in the

Opposite: a vegan dog, shortly before he went into a retreat

Cheesy explains the finer points of a territorial claim

summer months, and only then when weather conditions are near perfect. I boarded the launch off Ballinskelligs pier, legendary landing place for several survivors of the flood in (suspicious precision here) 2958 BC, when Noah's son Bith and two other stalwarts, Ladra and Fintan, landed with forty-nine women including Noah's daughter, Cessair. When Bith and Ladra died, presumably of exhaustion, the lone survivor Fintan understandably did a runner, leaving Cessair, who loved him, to die of a broken heart. I don't know, men.

As the launch pulled away, I watched two little black and white figures, still bemused by the incoming tide, disappear as we headed out to sea.

'You're lucky,' said Joe, ex-lighthouse keeper and owner of the boat, as we powered through the deep green swell of the Atlantic under a cloudless sky. 'We don't get many days like this.'

The other three passengers, all French and immaculately clothed in designer oilskins, gradually took on the colour of the surrounding ocean as the small boat rose and fell like an elevator. As with a lot of men on that part of the coast, Joe followed the seasons. In the summer he fished and ran people out to the Skelligs. During the storm-bound winter months he worked on building sites in London.

'How can you ever live in London?' he asked. It was a question I often asked myself, particularly on a day like this off the Irish coast.

As we approached Little Skellig, a jagged shard of weather-stained sandstone rising sheer out of the ocean, thousands of gannets rose and wheeled and dived about us, sometimes plunging from a height of a hundred feet or more. The island is the second largest gannetry in the world, with upwards of twenty thousand pairs so closely packed they created an illusion of drifting snow on the crevices from a blizzard of birds whirling above. The noise was so great we had to shout to be heard as we passed close by rocks sculpted into fantastic shapes by the unimaginable seas of the winter storms that had been known to smash the lighthouse on the Great Skellig, 175 feet above them.

The panorama of the surrounding ocean had expanded now, to take in the Blasket Islands fifteen miles to the north and Puffin Island and Bull Rock to the south. All around us oceanic seabirds that would never see the mainland swooped and soared, while ahead only Skellig Michael stood between us and Newfoundland, three

The gannetry of Little Skellig

thousand miles away. Memories of my brief encounter with the
Merchant Navy inevitably surfaced, and promptly submerged, as
Skellig Michael loomed into view. A number of puffins escorted
us in like self-important little businessmen as we approached the
tiny, dangerous quay, appropriately known as Blind Man's Cove.
Now uninhabited, it looked as remote and desolate as the end of the
world, which is what it must have seemed in the Dark Ages. Then,
it was inhabited by small groups of monks, never more than twelve,
who created an extraordinary monastic settlement six hundred feet
above the sea on the one small strip of level ground on the rock:
six beehive cells and two small oratories constructed of unmortared
stone, still intact after fourteen hundred years of Atlantic weather.
How the monks survived is not known, but as I negotiated my way
around the bedlam of nesting kittiwakes at Cross Cove, and climbed
the near vertical stairway hewn into the rock, the question I asked
myself was, why?

Was it, as some modern theologians have argued, a highly visible expression of the power of the will? A compelling example of the ability of the comparatively new religion to inspire these men to triumph over nature and themselves and show their contempt for the material world? A brilliant exercise in public relations to win hearts and minds at a time when the early Christian church had little economic power and few powerful military allies? Or were these monks indulging in spiritual pastimes familiar still in many of the world's religions – solitude, self-mortification, meditation – in order to gain through mystical experience a deeper insight into a life which at that time was particularly nasty, brutish and short? Or did they come to this, the most difficult and desolate outpost of them all, in an excess of eremetical zeal that was sweeping Ireland at that time, simply because it was perceived to be just that? Whatever the motives, Skellig Michael stands as an extreme example of the desire for a certain kind of experience that still draws people, as it always has, to what was once the edge of the world.

Certainly it had drawn me. And standing there above the monastery, on the steep slope of the highest point of this rock on the edge of Europe, I came across a synchronicity that almost gave me a mystical experience.

It became the custom for a while for lovers to sail out to the Great Skellig to pledge their troth to each other. Nature was inclined to take its course in the close confines of the boats, and gossip eventually put paid to the custom. But not before a namesake of mine made a visit with his beloved. My mother was a Connolly, a clan that originated in Munster, of which Kerry is part. And, standing on the slope, I looked down and saw, set in the rock in small white stones, C.P. Connolly and A. Callan 1841. They were the only names inscribed anywhere on the rock. I would like to think they made love, on the kind of day I was experiencing, and that the fruits of their labours, on the eve of the Great Famine that changed Ireland forever, led directly to my returning to the same spot 149 years later. But then, the Great Skellig does have a way of exciting the imagination, as I'm sure those intrepid monks once discovered when all the world was young. As if to add to the occasion, as we left the Great Skellig, set in waters over 250 feet deep, a small school of whales sailed majestically by,

Skellig Michael: synchronicity and silence

heading out into the green clear depths of the last true wilderness in the Western world.

Arriving back at Ballinskelligs Bay, I was greeted by my two acolytes who had presumably spent the day in solitude, self-mortification (I forgot to feed them before I left) and meditation in an attempt to gain a deeper insight into the eternal mystery of tides. Amid the usual scramble, gulps and growls of feeding time, I posed a question to them which the Skellig monks may often have asked themselves.

'Do you think we have any part to play in the scheme of things?'

Pugwash belched. Cheesy farted.

'Was that a yes or a no?'

I suppose cats don't really need to consider the deeper mysteries of life. Their entire lives are one big bloody mystery.

6

Dingle's Enigma Variations

The weather had taken a turn for the normal on the Dingle peninsula, my new base for exploring the west of Ireland and the route my mother's family had taken to eventual emigration. So had the Incorrigibles – again.

'It couldn't have been a dog fish or something like that, could it? Oh no. It had to be the bloody lobster, didn't it?'

The Fagin and the Artful Dodger of the cat world, working their inimitable double act, had struck again. A party of French scuba divers had returned to the small cove where we were camped with a fair haul. In pride of place among it was one large lobster. As we celebrated with a few glasses of wine, the prize was ceremonially boiled and left to cool. I should have known. As Pugwash did the rounds to receive a stroke – known in military circles as a diversionary tactic – Cheesy moved in on the main target. Cries of *Merde!* raised the alarm, but too late. The evidence lay scattered under the camper and it took several hours in the nearest pub to re-establish the *entente cordiale*.

'Five people, four rounds, at one pound fifty a pint. Do you know how much you've cost me, you – comedians?' The seminar on home economics fell on defiantly deaf ears as guilt (if any) was busily purged by a good wash.

As for the weather, the light breezes and soft summer days suddenly disappeared with a vengeance as we arrived on the peninsula. First came a dense fog which set the scene for a place that rather prides itself on twilight Celtic mystery. As I took the road out of Dingle through Ventry and on towards Slea Head, clochans – ancient beehive huts – loomed out of fog on the lower slopes of Mount Eagle like creatures from a fifties horror movie. Although a few are mysteriously lined with Bronze Age breeze blocks and held together by neolithic cement, the majority – over four hundred – are authentic. This area

The weather had taken a turn for the normal

has one of the greatest concentrations of ancient remains in Europe, with clochans, ogham stones, promontory forts, ring forts, ruined monasteries, early churches and oratories, including that perfectly preserved masterpiece, the Gallarus Oratory.

The layers of visible history in what is still one of the most isolated parts of Ireland combine with a wild and empty landscape to create the mood of a place that seems even now to be outside the mainstream of the late twentieth century. If the ancient remains are a tangible echo of race memory, the land itself reflects the ever present sea. There is a peculiar fluidity about the treeless landscape: while the green and grey bare rounded mountains echo the Atlantic swell, the headlands sweep up towards the coast like a petrified wave before crashing down to the shore line in a chaos of weathered sandstone. If the landscape is operatic, it's Wagner rather than Mozart, and you half expect to see a large blonde appear from behind a rock – Erda, the Earth mother, probably – and start warbling at Wotan to leave her ring alone, while a chorus drones on about knowing what fear is.

Part of the unique mood of the Dingle peninsula is an immensely long and complex cultural history set in a place virtually empty now of people. The small scattered communities are rarely more than a hundred or so and Dingle itself with a population of twelve hundred feels more like a village than a town, although one great advantage of this is that local tourism – 'Like the sex', said one local wag pointedly – is in its infancy. Which is probably why Funghi the Dingle dolphin is a major industry, prompting interminable odes from ecologically sound poets, a small fleet of redundant fishing boats which must give the poor mammal a headache as they constantly run sightseers out to his playground, and a flood of trashy spin-offs that would probably have Kylie and Jason grinding their perfect teeth. 'Funghi the fucking Dolphin' as one piece of irritated graffiti put it is, however, the exception, although perhaps a sign of things to come when the new multi-million – and much contested – marina is completed.

If Dingle town is the future, Ballyferriter, towards the western end of the peninsula, is firmly traditional. The pubs still combine the services of a corner shop, and the shops themselves are long dark canyons of tinned goods that help see the locals through the harsh winters devoid of fresh fruit and vegetables. A crowd of men left evening mass and made a bee-line for the local pub and the television set brought in for the occasion: the first round of the World Cup. It was England versus Ireland and I followed them in, curious to soak up the World Cup fever that was sweeping Ireland and had so far eluded me. That was my first mistake. This area is part of the Gaeltacht, and as I stood at the bar surrounded by Gaelic-speaking locals I felt, for the first time in Ireland, very very English. A feeling that rapidly intensified as the match got under way. Every ball possession by Ireland was greeted by a roar of approval and loud excited commentary. Every pass by England was met with a stony silence. The dot-dash of noise and silence continued through the first half like Morse code, and the message was loud and clear: this was no ordinary football match. History was being played out on the small screen, and several hundred years of chickens were coming home to roost. There was a flurry of activity on the screen and then – England scored. 'Yeah!' I yelled, half rising out of my chair and punching the air. That was my second mistake. A profound silence descended on the bar and every head in the room turned slowly in my direction. I felt like Julian Clary walking into a wild west saloon full of men who were inclined to do what a man has to do. I decided not to.

'Sure is a hell of a game, this football, yes *sir!*' I said in my best American accent, to no one in particular, and a roomful of Celtic heads swivelled back to the screen as play resumed.

Minutes later Ireland equalized and my ear-drums imploded under the impact of a huge roar that verged on hysteria. That the final whistle saw the match end in a draw was irrelevant. Not a soul in the place saw it as other than a great victory. I staggered out into the night a deafer and wiser man.

The English may be responsible for much of modern Irish history and politics, but it was the Celts who left a lasting legacy with the Irish and through them with Western European culture, history, and politics. The remnants of that gypsy empire, then in the twilight of its day, arrived here around 350 BC and Ireland became the last territory they ever conquered. Haunted and disturbed by the stone remains of earlier settlers and threatened by their beliefs, they re-created the ghosts as part of their own mythology . . . a tradition which still continues in Northern Ireland.

Untroubled by invaders until the Vikings arrived in the eighth century, they had the time to fuse imagination with existing skills that brought their art to a high point and established the clan system from which the Irish people emerged. There were about 150 kin groups which never did manage to amalgamate, as anyone walking down the Kilburn High Road around closing time will verify. Each had a king whose timetable makes some of the increasingly Wagnerian members of the royal family look like workaholics. The ancient law of the Crith Gablach defined his occupation. Sunday – drinking ale. Monday – legal business. Tuesday – chess. Wednesday – greyhound racing. Thursday – marital intercourse. Friday – horse racing. Saturday – judgements. This Andy Capp lifestyle, still familiar in my home town on North Humberside – although Thursdays are now optional and Saturday judgements usually reserved for football – underlined a fundamental transformation: the move from the matricentred society of the Bronze Age Picts to the patriarchal warrior-dominated society of the Celts. If the foundation of patriarchy rests upon the insecurity of men in the process of procreation and a profound sense of alienation, sometimes during and often after our small contribution, it was the Celts who helped introduce and spread the ersatz substitute which still plagues modern Ireland and indeed the Western world. Out of it have come a whole constellation of attitudes and strategies familiar in any office, staff room, and similar war zone: the male of the species determined to reassure himself and everybody else that he really does matter in the scheme of things. The Celtic warrior, who set the bench mark for football hooligans for ever more, tended to be prosaic about these matters. Before battle they spent time alone simulating birth pangs, and afterwards slept with the gory head of the enemy between their legs, as a not too subtle reminder that birth through death was the way forward. With the Celts, fatherhood arrived with a vengeance and things would never be the same again. And from the Middle East to Northern Ireland the same old propaganda still prevails. The lives of the future are safeguarded through death, not birth, and to die for one's cause is a far far better thing, while to give birth is merely a biological function.

Such was the legacy of the irascible Celtic nation beloved of New Age believers, of which a number have settled in this area; all of them enthusiastically extolling the virtues of a more peaceful time.

If the landscape is littered with the remains of a past that shaped the present, the people today are moulded by the land and water, as I discovered, parked by Dunmore Head, the most westerly point on the Irish mainland. I went paddling in a small cove while the reincarnations of two Celtic hooligans watched nervously from the beach. Maybe they have a built-in barometer in their formidable survival kit, because within hours the weather changed again. A full gale blew up, driving first a heavy green swell before it and then lines of breakers on to the rocks below with a thunderous hiss of white noise. The entire cove became an inferno of cross seas, turning it into a giant jacuzzi. Little wonder the Spanish ship that ran aground there in 1982 stood little chance, adding yet another victim to the long casualty list of the Blasket Sound offshore.

As spray spattered the camper a hundred feet above the wreck,

Cheesy enjoys a character-forming gale

mist crept down the flanks of Mount Eagle and squalls of rain swept horizontally across the headland. The Incorrigibles were distinctly unimpressed.

'It's character-forming,' I said as yet another huge breaker exploded on to the rocks below and more spray swept over us. Cats have no sense of adventure.

As I stood watching the show, an old man festooned in oilskins that flapped in the wind and made him look like some large prehistoric bird came by driving a small herd of cows.

'Bit of a breeze,' said this veteran of a thousand storms, who turned out to be the owner of Dunmore Head. Now the Blasket Islands just offshore are deserted – they were evacuated in 1953 – his little cottage is the last occupied house before America. His name was Sean Bigley, and he was, I suppose, The Last Man In Europe.

Sean had lived there all his life and his family had owned the land for generations. I asked him how things had changed.

Sean Bigley, the last man in Europe

'If you had come here in the fifties there was no motor car then and everything was by the horse. What my life was then was what my father's had been and his before. But now everything is changing. If I took the horse into Dingle now, he'd be flummoxed by it all.'

Change might confuse his horses, but I had the impression that Sean had a certain amount of iron in the soul and was disinclined to let the twentieth century walk over him. One weapon against tourists who might feel the need to wander was several boards warning of poisoned land. I told him that in Britain infecting the land was done courtesy of the government. He thought I was joking. He obviously hadn't heard of little John Gummer, patron saint of farmers.

This is a Gaelic-speaking area and its speech rhythms inflect the

Sheep ruminate where tourists fear to tread

spoken English. Listening to Sean, I was reminded that a few miles away on the Blasket Islands, several fine books originated from Islanders giving accounts of daily lives unchanged but on the point of changing. One of them, an old and by then blind woman called Peig Sayers, said: 'I see myself here, sitting on the fence, looking around me and thinking on a hundred things a gone, and I see the change that has come into life in my own memory . . . An alternative life's being led. It can't be helped, I suppose. Life changing as the years passing along.'

Shortly afterwards, it all changed forever, and the islands were emptied.

With an improvement in the weather we moved to another, more exposed cove where the still heavy swell swept directly in on to the beach and the hiss and sigh of the surf lulled even my two paranoids into sociability.

Returning from a long cycle ride, I freewheeled down the steep road on the flank of Mount Eagle that led to the cove. Applying the brakes at the crucial moment produced an ominous ping, and salt-corroded brake cable twanged past my ear. As I careered past several tourists and two preening cats, someone shouted: 'I think there is no road any more.'

'I know that!' I yelled, as I shot on to the beach, hit a sand dune and somersaulted into a tangled heap. Feeling like the original big girl's blouse, I looked up to see the tourists taking photographs while the Incorrigibles, miffed at a temporary shift in the limelight, wandered off to annihilate anything small in fur or feathers.

'I think he had trouble with his brakes,' announced the Megaphone – again. Men like this start wars.

Later, as I sat by the camper removing sand and applying Dettol, I had time to watch the child that invariably emerges in the adult when the surf is up. Little old ladies in saggy elasticated cozzies with big flowers on them and what looked like giant inverted tulips on their heads ran coquettishly in and out of the water shrieking girlishly. A middle-aged man made little hops with both feet together as he skimmed stones and yelled 'Yee – haar'. He wore a three-piece suit and tight shiny shoes and looked like a solicitor which, given some of the solicitors I have known, he probably was. Throughout the day the light changed over the sea, transmuting it from emerald to turquoise to silver while the clouds shadow-danced across the mountains. After a while the scale of the place seemed manageable – and then you saw another person in the distance, swallowed up in the immensity of the landscape. On a warm summer's day the peninsula was magnificent. But in the winter it must be a wild and desolate place.

On a Friday evening, the isolated pub cum general store near the cove provided a focus for the local community to come together at an impromptu ceilidh. It was a place for music and gossip and talk of the week's doings and that essential renewing of the strands of friendship and shared experience that binds a community together.

I think there is no road any more

The very sparseness of the population was likely to intensify such bonds. Friendship in these places, as Peig Sayers said, 'was like a little rose in the wilderness'.

By midnight, the roses were beginning to wilt. While the musicians, several sheets to the wind, managed to argue and almost keep in tune at the same time, two groups exploring the efficacy of non-violence as a policy in Northern Ireland were about to adopt the Arnold Schwarzenegger strategy for peaceful co-existence. Basically this involved going outside in pairs and thumping each other until they both fell down, then getting up and shaking hands. It seemed to work, too, judging by the camaraderie at the bar immediately afterwards. The exception was a man who had introduced himself earlier as a poet, and kept sticking a large knife into the table next to me, as poets will, whenever he wanted to emphasize a point. Several women had new babies with them, and large white breasts loomed from the dark corner by the fire from time to time as night feeds made their demands. Other young children ran among the tables, and it was appropriate that my two, invited in earlier by the young landlord Padraig, enthusiastically joined in the anarchy that was the weekly celebration of a community. And having survived the vicissitudes of famine, poverty, mass migration and wild Atlantic weather, it was a community that might well survive the onslaught of modern tourism. As dawn back-lit Mount Brandon, I waltzed two dozy but deeply contented cats into the camper and left them to sleep it off. It was probably my imagination plus several pints of Guinness, but at such times, the past rose up, ghosts danced, and the twentieth century faded into the shadows.

7

Sex and Pugs and Rock 'n' Roll

Following the flight path of the maternal side of the family, I was struck by their unerring ability to seek out the most desolate and inhospitable parts of western Ireland as they travelled north. This could be due of course to an incurably poetic nature – or an incurable optimism bound up with a profound ignorance of Irish geography and sheer bloody-mindedness. On the other hand, they might have been plain unlucky.

It was, according to the locals, the mad season when we arrived on the Burren in County Clare: the middle of summer when pubs reach a theoretical closing time while it's still broad daylight, and bonfires are lit on St John's Eve – a Christian festival grafted on to something much older – to ward off the evil ones who are supposedly thick on the ground at this time of year. They may be right. Glancing out of the camper window, I could see two at that very moment, lounging about the Doolin camp site ever hopeful of a handout.

'Would it help if I provided a couple of hungry and homeless placards?' I suggested. There was of course no response. Sarcasm is wasted on cats.

Mad because seasonal visitors were now arriving in this, the most sparsely populated area in Ireland, bringing with them a variety of urban psychoses to liven the passing days – and nights. Mad in particular though when Ireland achieved yet another draw in the World Cup. 'God alone knows what would happen to Ireland if we won,' said Sean behind the bar of O'Connor's pub as the audience in green, white and orange performed a limited Brazilian wave in front of the specially installed television set and the bonfire for St John's Eve went up in flames prematurely as Ireland scored.

The Irish, it has to be said, know how to have a good time, and here in the tiny hamlet of Doolin, with its three legendary pubs

that have made it a mecca of traditional Irish music, the ceilidh has evolved into a kind of perfection. Too perfect, some locals argue, as visitors sit reverently in O'Connor's, robbing the occasion of an essential ingredient: the crack.

'Irish music is not supposed to be listened to sitting down. It's for standing up and walking around and talking against and dancing to,' the youthful owner of the Doolin camp site, who favoured an alternative setting – Mcgann's – stated firmly. And in Mcgann's, all this was possible, frequently, and with a much younger crowd which, to a young local male with a love life on a restricted diet, might have been a deciding factor. Whatever the choice of venue, even the most cloth-eared visitors found themselves singing their way home or sitting on a dry stone wall warbling on a tin whistle as they watched the sun set over the Aran Islands.

Other light entertainment included the occasional old gaffer who spoke only in aphorisms tried and tested on a generation of visitors seduced by the prevailing atmosphere.

'You only need three things to enter the gates of heaven,' said one to a group of entranced Irish-Americans. 'Love tenderly, walk humbly, and always think the best of your neighbour.'

Which makes a change from back home in south London, where they tend to love gingerly, walk quickly, and wisely assume that even if you are paranoid, it doesn't mean they're not out to get you.

The delights of this part of the world are lost, of course, on the Incorrigibles. They too are prone to sitting on stone walls while the sun sets, but mainly because it gets dark afterwards, which is when their particular entertainment begins. I'm inured to finding a sad little row of mouse tails neatly laid out on the floor of the camper every morning. Even so, finding the bottom half of a rabbit standing surreally by the fridge after a particularly lively night in Mcgann's pub was enough to put anybody off their muesli.

'You'll notice many Irish dogs are muzzled,' I said to the Burke and Hare of the cat world as they sprawled complacently beside their trophy. 'Don't tempt me.'

Doolin, the morning after

Quite apart from the nagging thought that I might be next, it may take some explaining if they graduate to sheep.

If Doolin attracts traditional music aficionados from all over Ireland and beyond, the Burren attracts another sort of visitor: often large, usually gregarious and with the kind of legs that stride forever over the roughest terrain. They usually go with the kind of voice that causes landslides and come in many accents. When I was a child, no Cubs' den or Brownie pack seemed complete without one. I met several pounding across the extraordinary landscape in search of rare plants or Stone Age burial monuments, and they provided a human perspective for a place that would otherwise seem to be not of this earth. A combination of Carboniferous limestone, glaciation, deforestation and centuries of weathering have created its hundred square miles and there is nothing quite like it. Cromwell's surveyor, Ludlow, ever pragmatic, called it: 'A savage land, yielding neither

Burke and Hare wait for night to fall

water enough to drown a man, nor a tree to hang him by, nor soil enough to bury him.' Quite.

Burren in Gaelic means rocky land, and this massive plateau of limestone absorbs the rain effortlessly. Several hundred miles of cave systems, many still unexplored, have been created by the underground rivers. The monolithic expanses of terraces, bone-white or steel-grey, depending upon the light, are scoured of soil on the upper reaches and yet provide the most unlikely home for one of Europe's finest collections of Arctic, alpine, and Mediterranean plants which thrive uniquely side by side in the cracks and grooves of the weathered limestone. Hence all those big legs. The Burren is never out of bloom, although at its best in the spring and early summer when over a thousand species, from gentians to orchids, pull in the enthusiasts.

I naively imagined anyone wandering the trackless waste of limestone would have their navigation sorted. Apparently not, judging by the waifs and strays I occasionally came across. Prominent among them was a lone Dutchman, who had misplaced his entire family and like his fictional alter ego seemed doomed to wander the earth for eternity. Having arranged to meet them at a crossroads that seemed to exist on paper, he claimed the meeting point had stubbornly refused to materialize. And as he searched the Green road, a wide ancient track for livestock that ran across the top of the Burren, desperation was clearly mounting. Not only had he mislaid his mother, wife and two children, but he also carried the car keys and that day's food. Whatever the outcome, this man was going to get it in the neck from all sides, hence the paranoia. 'What if they have fallen in a bog?' he worried, scanning the bleak landscape with old-fashioned World War Two binoculars.

'I shouldn't think so. The Burren's about the only place in Ireland without one.'

'Maybe they have been attacked by animals?'

'Sheep?'

And so on. Despite the rhetoric of the government, sometimes at least, a man and his family were not easily parted. All of this highlighted a major (and probably the sole) advantage of travelling with two cats. When the little buggers got lost, it was merely a question of waiting until feeding time. Wherever they were, whatever the circumstances, regardless of the terrain, nothing on earth, and certainly nothing in Ireland, would prevent them turning up on cue to claim their divinely allotted place in the food chain.

Regardless, if the Burren was a botanist's dream and a potholer's delight, it was a cat's worst nightmare. Of all the places we had visited, this was the least popular with the Incorrigibles. Inveterate agoraphobics, the endless expanse of sculptured rock had them trudging warily from one Stone Age burial site to another, sniffily inspecting each one with all the enthusiasm of a British Prime Minister almost anywhere in Western Europe.

The Doolin camp site was something else. Large expanses of soft sand, the kind of attention from the mainly young music fans usually reserved for star musicians, and an endless supply of small mammals had done wonders to restore their faith in travelling. What it had done

The Burren: a remarkable landscape . . .

and (opposite) a cat's worst nightmare

for the local small mammal population was another matter. Having abandoned any attempt to expose the homicidal twosome to some of the finer points of survival in a hostile world, I joined forces with a musician friend from Brittany.

André was the kind of guy who could make the stones weep with his guitar, but even his own mother denied all knowledge of him when he'd had a few. A fine musician with a death wish that narrowly avoided fulfilment most weekends, he was a man who believed fervently in the here and now and left the future to the tender mercies of politicians and accountants. A neglect of the latter explained André's residence in Ireland.

'You're a natural Buddhist,' I said, referring to his ability to live entirely in the present, as we drove out to the legendary Spancil Hill fair near Ennis.

'You mean I am a fat bastard, eh?'

'That too, André, that too.'

The fair is held once a year, and now only for a day, but horse dealers come from all over Ireland to buy and sell anything from expensive hunters to spavined has-beens. New Age wanderers pose self-consciously by quaint traditional caravans that your average traveller wouldn't be seen dead in, while farmers and horse traders of every kind congregate for the real business of the day, creating a scene that has probably changed little over the centuries. Haggling takes forever, with the seller adopting the initial position that this is the finest horseflesh since Red Rum, and the buyer pointing out that it probably won't make it back to the stable and it would be kindest to put it out of its misery. Eventually a sale is arrived at and a third party bears witness as they spit on their hands and shake on the deal. Something atavistic stirred as I watched the action, and I remembered my maternal grandfather describing just such a scene which his own grandfather had witnessed. I felt as well as saw the continuum, as hordes of children swarmed about the negotiations while those not dealing played pitch and toss or find the lady, or simply marinated in the only real building on the site, a cavernous pub called Brohan's.

Returning to Doolin via Lisdoonvarna acquainted us with another ancient but still thriving custom. In the past, the isolation of the area made it difficult for nature to take its course in the normal haphazard way, and single men and women had to resort to more structured methods. Out of necessity grew an annual month-long matchmaking festival held, pragmatically, in September, after the harvest was in. The festival still thrives, reflecting the sparseness of the local population and the basic needs of single people everywhere, although these days the festival caters mainly for those taking a more positive view of a mid-life crisis. In June, the various pubs which host the festival were empty, although they still looked as if Barbara Cartland's interior decorator ran amok as she wrote the menus. Hearts and flowers proliferated, while the Honeymoon Special featured in one tavern turned out to be (Freudian overtones here) a banana split.

André, whose libido deserves a place in the Guinness Book of Records, was fascinated by the mating rituals of western Ireland. As we examined the wall to wall photographs of couples who had played the ultimate round of bingo and clutched gamely at each other while optimistically calling house, he wondered aloud at the peculiar chemistry of Lisdoonvarna.

'Look at this one 'ere, 'e look like the Elephant Man. 'Ow did she pick 'im?'

'Who can fathom the mystery of the human heart, André?'

Certainly not André, who sounds like the presenter of Rapido, and on a good day looks like a haystack by Monet. Despite this, there were times after playing a gig when he seemed to have been marinated in pheromones, given the reaction of the women in the audience. Seeing him emerge from his nearby tent with yet another starry-eyed fan after – judging by the late night soundtrack – enthusiastically exploring the A to Z of that seminal work by Alex Joy on The Comfort of Sex, I wondered how he was coping with the post-AIDS world.

'I hope you practise safe sex, André.'

'Yes, I am practising all the time,' he answered with ominous ambiguity.

Leaving the environs of the matchmakers, André and I decided to relax at Ireland's only spa, on the outskirts of Lisdoonvarna, specializing in hot sulphur baths.

'Who knows,' I said, 'it might moderate those pheromones.'

Judging by the end result, it may have.

'We 'ave come out of thees smelling like a giant fart,' pronounced

André as we emerged. He had a point. That night in an invariably packed Doolin pub, we found ourselves creating our own space as the cordon sanitaire of bad eggs percolated through to the surrounding throng. As I smiled winningly at some Americans edging away, André helped them along with sotto voce comments such as: 'I think, my friend, it is time for your annual bath, eh?' I idly wondered what the sentence was in Ireland for justifiable homicide, but then he began to play. As he sang a very old and beautiful Breton folk song, I wasn't quite sure if the tears in some of the audience's eyes were an emotional release or the price of a particularly sensitive sense of smell.

The following day I met another musician who for many of my generation helped provide a brief musical highlight of their adolescence. Of all the groups that emerged in the sixties, it was the Jimi Hendrix Experience that found its time precisely. Noel Redding laid down the bass riffs that underpinned the pyrotechnics of Mitch Mitchell's drumming and the sublime free-form guitar of Hendrix. Noel had returned to live in Ireland seventeen years ago and I met up with him in nearby Ballyvaughan, where he was playing a gig with his partner Carol. This was the year of the 'big death', as Noel called it, and the record industry would be churning out the back catalogue of CDs to commemorate the death of Hendrix in 1970. Noel, however, as a casualty of an industry that excelled in devouring its young, would not receive a penny from it all, and the title of the forthcoming autobiography, *Are You Experienced?*, had an ironic ring to it.

It was a familiar sixties saga. Noel was a working class kid, inspired by the first wave of rock and roll that swept across from an America that was already a never never land of adolescent icons from Dean to Presley, leather jackets to Levis. An end-of-the-rainbow country in a grey, post-war world of baggy suits, mild and bitter and Woodbines, America colonized the imagination of Britain's youth in the late fifties and early sixties with its glittering mythology of sexual promise and rebellion. And if the sixties was a time of complex social change made simple by adolescent idealism, the music was a perfect soundtrack. All over the country boys picked up guitars and wish-fulfilled themselves into musicians, and I never have met a man of my generation who didn't harbour a secret desire to do the same in his early teens. Noel

Redding's particular experience was to have every teenage boy's dream fulfilled beyond his wildest expectations, only to have it turn into a nightmare which, judging from our conversation, still casts a long shadow. After a brief stint of earning his dues with makeshift bands, a chance, almost casual encounter with Hendrix in 1966 led to the forming of the Jimi Hendrix Experience, and things would never be the same again. The group provided a musical focus for the late sixties' mood of hedonism, and lived out the appropriate life style to the point of extinction and, in the case of Hendrix, beyond. Four years later it was all over, the group had self-destructed, Hendrix was dead, burned out like a supernova, and Noel was left to pick up the pieces and try to make some sense of what happened. He's still trying, although his book may have helped to lay a few personal ghosts to rest. If the mythology of rock is littered with victims and sundry basket cases, there are a surprising number of survivors. Among them is Noel. After the three-ring circus of sex and drugs and rock and roll that made up the everyday life of the sixties super-groups, it came as a mild surprise to find him still standing. I asked him why he was there.

'I came to Ireland in 1973 when things were really bad. Trouble with contracts and the Hendrix estate, trouble with the boys in blue and chemical substances. In fact I'm still wary about going back to London on that score. A lot of bad stuff just coming at me, and I needed to get my head together. The first year here was really hard, and in the end I was so broke I signed away all claims to money from the Hendrix estate for . . . well, for peanuts, looking back on it. If I knew what I know now, I'd be very well off. As it is . . .'

As it was, he bought a place in Clonakilty and gradually put himself back together. Clearly the Hendrix experience had left its mark, but the man's sense of humour, his partner in life, and his music had pulled him through, and still did.

'Now Carol and I play most days, and that's important to me. What I found out living here is that playing music is the only thing that really counts. The rest is bullshit. Otherwise, Carol and I live down in Cork with a bit of land, three dogs, eight cats (blanch) and a goat, and it's grand. Ireland's the kind of place to find yourself, mate, and what I found was, music's my life. It always was.'

I liked Noel. He'd found his space and he'd found his place, as they say, with the tenacity of a born survivor. I introduced him to another one: Cheesy. They got on just fine. I guess it takes one to know one.

Back in Doolin, another generation was finding itself, too, and I was not surprised that after ten years of computerized pap written by committees there was a revival of interest in music from earlier decades, which was once again finding its way into current musical trends. Popular music always has been good at expressing the mood of its time and reflecting prevailing values and attitudes. I suppose in that respect each generation gets the music it deserves.

On the camp site André was sleeping off the previous night's labours, and two small black and white figures were watching the sun set over Inisheer. They both sat on a stone wall with ears pointed forward, as cats will when something has their undivided attention. Perhaps they were contemplating the blank limestone sheet of the Burren, written on in stone by countless generations as a testament to tenacity and the will to survive. Or perhaps they were considering that history is merely a part of a continuum, and any perception of it relative to the present. But when I looked over the wall, my reverie ended. Several young rabbits, who were unlikely to get much older, were happily bouncing about while Burke and Hare patiently waited for night to fall. Some things never change.

Noel Redding, with another born survivor

8

Luminous Virgins for Sale

'Ireland is a country of uneven surface and rather watery.' Not a lot has changed since Giraldus wrote about his travels in Ireland in the twelfth century. Of course, he didn't have a pair of alternative comedians travelling with him with a distinct taste for anarchy and a profound disregard for (my) personal safety. Pugwash continued to muffle the airways as I drove along while Cheesy lounged across my shoulder as flatulent and vociferous as ever. To keep a marginal peace I rarely drove at more than forty miles an hour, although at the best of times Irish roads are a great incentive to long slow drives. On any one road, a state-of-the-art four-lane highway can suddenly turn into a country lane with a surface like an overdone pizza. Road signs can also concentrate the mind wonderfully. Leaving aside the local adolescent sport of turning them around to face in the wrong direction, and accepting that miles and kilometres are interchangeable, distances themselves are a moveable feast sometimes. Thirty miles, announces a sign, and ten miles on another announces thirty-five on the same road in the same direction. Enquiries about distances tend to be more reliable once you have cracked the code. 'Just round the corner' is usually two miles. 'A bit down the road' is never less than five, and if they say 'a fair way' take sandwiches and a flask.

All of this of course had taken its toll on the camper. Exploding tyres, imploding camshafts and a disintegrating exhaust system that made me sound like a World War Two landing craft had all contributed to the expanding wallets of garages across Ireland, not to mention a profound sense that life is transitory, and chaos, as with the universe, a basic law of travel. On the other hand, I was on first name terms with the Irish AA. As yet another loud bang and shower of shredded rubber signalled an exploding tyre to the locals, and nearby garages no doubt optimistically pricked up their ears in anticipation, Cheesy added another hole to the ozone layer. Changing the tyre with practised ease, I noticed we were close to Knock, perhaps Ireland's most famous shrine and a place where miracles are said to occur on a regular basis. Given the comments at the last garage about the state of the camper, I was definitely in the market for one.

Knock itself consists mainly of the Basilica and shrine and a street of remarkable shops geared to the pilgrim trade. In 1879 on a wet August evening, fifteen people are said to have witnessed an apparition of Mary, Joseph and St John before a cross with the Lamb by the gable end of the local church. Two commissions and a visit from the Pope later, a local industry has blossomed which includes a heavily subsidized airport, a rest house and hostel, St Brendan's

A Knock shop

restaurant, St Anne's bar and – my favourite – St Gerard's take-away. As some pilgrims topped up with holy water from the many taps by the shrine, using containers that ranged from little plastic Marys to gallon containers for family sized miracles, others paid their respects to the shrine inside a large glass box.

It was the Knock shops, however, that caught my attention, with one of the finest collections of kitsch this side of those shops in Belgravia that cater for clients from the Middle East. Amid a

A resting actor . . .

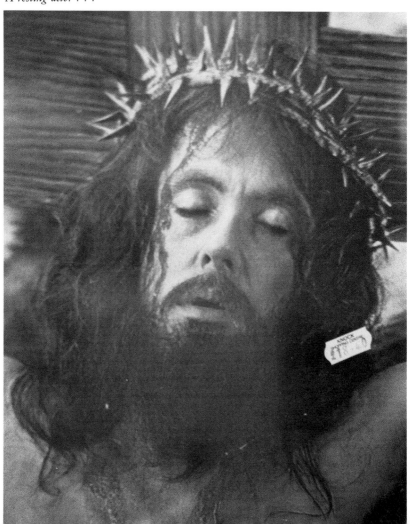

distinctive smell of plastic and acetate, garishly detailed statues of
saints – 'easily washable' announced the shop's owner as I browsed
– competed with posed photographs. Among these was a particular
favourite: a touched-up portrait of an actor making ends meet by
hanging dolefully from a cross with eyes that opened and shut as
you walked by.

'We sell an awful lot of these to the Belgians,' said the shop owner
hopefully as I swayed from side to side in front of the photograph to

makes ends meet

get the full effect. 'Of course,' she continued as I moved regretfully on, 'the luminous virgins are always very popular.' Ah, 'twas ever thus.

It was obviously a slow day. As I paused before a wall full of plaques with encouraging little homilies inscribed upon them in raised gold script, the owner made a final bid for a sale. 'Now a lot of men like to take one of these home,' she urged. I bet they do, I thought, as I read one which began: 'What is a mother?' and ended:

> 'Bless my little kitchen
> I love its every nook
> And bless me as I do my work
> And shop and wash and cook.'

Eat your heart out, Shirley Conran.

I wondered what the reaction might be if I presented one of these plaques to any of my women friends. Hanging dolefully from a cross with both eyes temporarily closed would probably be the least of my worries.

I finally bought several sticks of Knock rock and headed back to another pair of unbelievers beyond redemption.

'May you be in heaven a half hour before the devil knows you're dead,' said a sign ominously as I drove out of town. Fair enough.

Clattering on to a rather posh camp site near Sligo that evening, in an area that seems to include the name of Yeats in everything from crisps to toilet rolls, a loud clang announced the demise of the silencer. A small boy who may grow up to be a Nicholas Ridley announced to the entire camp site: 'His van's falling ta bits, look!' Sweet child. I introduced him to Cheesy. As the wails of a perforated young person subsided the camp site owner ambled out from the bar where they still appeared to be celebrating the triumphant draws of the World Cup. He eyed the van, with its occupants peering out balefully into the failing light of strange territory.

'Are you doing it for charity?' he asked finally.

'Got it in one.' It had been a long day.

However, it was not yet over. As happens on the road sometimes,

Miracles available, economy and family size

things took a turn for the better when four Dutch women pitched their huge tent next to the camper. Obviously members of the caring professions, they took one look at the van and invited us all in for a drink. They were in fact two couples and were still optimistically looking for women's clubs when they had met two Irish women, also partners, who put them right about the convoluted nature of sexual morality in Ireland. When the Irish couple joined us later and even Pugwash had reached saturation point with strokes, the conversation returned to the contradictory nature of the Irish. The Dutch women were all in their mid-twenties, came from Amsterdam and enlightened middle class backgrounds and had followed their sexual preference as a matter of course. The thought that such a personal matter could bring people into conflict with the law seemed to them ludicrous rather than oppressive.

They were having trouble with a country where the people are so spontaneous and free-spirited and disinclined to accept temporal authority on the one hand and yet live within the most rigid of conventional structures on the other. Just how rigid was made clear by the two Irish women. Both teachers, they lived and worked in small towns and their personal lives were mirror images of the Dutch women's. Any indication of their sexual preference would have meant the loss of everything else. One of them said it was a blessing she was not particularly attractive. I asked her why.

'People assume men are not interested in me, rather than the other way around.'

Her friend and partner, who was very attractive, agreed, saying she had invented several long-distance relationships over the years to keep the peace. Later, as I drifted off to sleep in the van, the animated conversation continued, punctuated with waves of laughter. I hoped the Irish women were storing up some good memories for the lean months ahead.

Arriving at the border the next day brought us for the first time into the dimension of Ireland that generally grabs the headlines. Nothing, though, had quite prepared me for the initial shock of the first

A one-way conversation in Knock

checkpoint. As we crawled gingerly over the speed ramps towards the armed RUC men and the heavily protected soldiers milling around the armoured installations, a convoy of squat ugly vehicles – aptly nicknamed Pigs – with a confidential telephone number stencilled on the sides to win hearts and minds, passed on the other side. It was an odd mixture of the strange and the familiar: images from a hundred news programmes brought to life on a bright summer's day. I felt as if I had walked into a film, with a depressingly familiar scenario.

As we were checked out, the Incorrigibles, as usual, provided the light relief. Pugwash roused himself and ambled over to the open window, unaware that men with guns rarely provide handouts to cats with an eating disorder. Meanwhile Cheesy lounged over my shoulder and chatted ingratiatingly with a stony-faced soldier in camouflage who did a Buster Keaton double-take.

'Is that – a cat?' he asked perceptively.

'Almost certainly.'

Pugwash purred hopefully.

'Two cats,' said the soldier, clearly officer material, as surprise mingled with suspicion in the RUC man's face. The familiar sound of a leaking balloon emerged from behind my left ear, and the combined might of the RUC and the British Army beat a hasty retreat.

'I'm sorry,' I explained. 'It's probably all the excitement.'

As Cheesy vented unselfconsciously, Pugwash, one of life's optimists, pulled out all the stops in his adorable cat routine. Lying flat on his back and kicking his legs in the air, he gazed upside down appealingly at potential donors.

'Don't you ever give up?' I muttered to one prostrate cat, and as they doubtfully waved us through I wondered what was going down on the computer. As we drove into another country, where they clearly did things differently, I tried to inject a note of caution into the proceedings.

'After all,' I said to the Incorrigibles, 'we could hardly have made more of an impact if we'd tap-danced our way across the border dressed as giant shamrocks and singing Molly Malone, could we?'

Pugsy Malone stretched luxuriously. His all-singing, all-dancing partner, Cheesy, bit my ear affectionately. Two innocents abroad in a strange land. That made three of us.

9

Croak Patrick

'If you think you understand the Irish question, you've been misinformed.' After a few days on the border, I was beginning to realize the wisdom of that comment. Travelling in the Republic, I had acquired a rather relaxed attitude to life in general and the Irish in particular. Within hours of crossing the border I had resurrected a host of knee-jerk responses which are useful in south London, but redundant in the west of Ireland. Now a familiar watchfulness and wariness had crept in, and just walking down a village street, or into a pub, was no longer a simple pleasure. It was a relief to be offered the use of a cottage in nearby Deserted Donegal, an apt name for an area that contained some magnificent empty beaches that put the Incorrigibles' agoraphobia into overdrive.

The cottage came as a shock after sharing the limited space of a Ford Transit camper with two fur-coated anarchists for several months. Suddenly there was an entire room just for living in, plus others for the exclusive exercises of sleeping, cooking and washing. The euphoria lasted just as long as it took the Incorrigibles to expand their territory into all the available space and attract a small tribe of local ragamuffins with pronounced Northern Irish calls. Exactly how the cat grapevine operates remains a mystery, but it certainly is effective. Within hours of our arrival, several strays were lounging about by the back door, and given their condition it was difficult to ignore them. As the feline equivalent of cardboard city grew outside, populated by abandoned, starving ferals, two large, well-fed specimens gazed benignly out from their warm, comfortable surroundings like National Theatre patrons driving across Waterloo Bridge in a Volvo.

I made the mistake of leaving a window open the next day as I left to explore the nearby village of Dunfanaghy and such ominously named places as Bloody Foreland and – worse – Tory Island. When I

Volvo cat, one owner, good runner, surveys the less fortunate

returned, the cottage looked like a Salvation Army hostel for down and out moggies, and the Incorrigibles had reserved the bedroom for their own exclusive use. Suffering the pangs of conscience familiar to Charing Cross commuters hurrying past the young beggars down the Strand, I gently deposited the protesting cats outside and re-directed the guilt at their overfed benefactors.

'As you know, I deplored the self-seeking, greed is good, screw you, I'm all right Jack philosophy of the eighties. But we must keep a sense of proportion, not confuse guilt with compassion, and observe the realities of everyday life. You are territorial, I am territorial. You are small, I am bigger. You cannot open a tin of cat food, I can. So, let us arrive at a compromise. I will invite my friends to stay in the cottage, you won't. My friends will eat inside, your friends will eat outside. I will sleep in the bedroom at night, you will not. Are we all absolutely clear on the living arrangements?'

The Incorrigibles, who know very little about the complexities of guilt, slept on.

Having parked them for a few days at the cottage, where they could explore their very own version of Glasnost without disrupting my sleep pattern, I returned to the border country with a mixture of mild relief and some trepidation. I had criss-crossed the border several times now and found the stop and search routine increasingly unnerving as the tension of the place seeped through like a stain. I was heading for Armagh again, as somewhere on the border with Monaghan was the place where the maternal side of my family had originated. As I waited to be checked out at Strabane, I wondered how long you had to live with this constant surveillance before it became merely routine. Perhaps because I had crossed several times now, each clearance took longer, the questions were more detailed, the friendly tone less reassuring, the guns casually pointed in my direction more difficult to ignore. Later, at another checkpoint, a soldier had a young dog with him which scrabbled excitedly around inside the van. Maybe he could smell the cats.

'I'm training him to be a sniffer dog,' he said, deadpan and perhaps joking. As they checked me out on the computer we made conversation.

'How long have you been out here?' I asked.

'Two and a half years.'

'I thought it was only four months?'

'It is.'

'He likes it, home from home,' said his mate.

I wondered what kind of home you had to come from to volunteer for eight consecutive tours of duty in Northern Ireland. Despite his easy manner, I felt uncomfortable with him. Putting yourself on the firing line day after day was hardly natural and in mid-conversation he had a habit of breaking off to stare into the middle distance at nothing in particular.

'What's it like in Ireland?' he asked suddenly.

'It's very beautiful,' I replied neutrally.

Checkpoint Charlies

'Yeah . . . I'd like to have a holiday there some time,' he said wist-fully, and we both knew he never would. In the present circumstances it would be suicidal. Clearance came and I started the van.

'Take care,' I said, and meant it. It was a hell of a way for a young man to be spending his youth.

'You take care, mate,' said his oppo, who had trained his gun on me throughout the conversation. 'We're the Professionals.'

'At what cost?' I wondered as I drove away.

I was graphically reminded of just how costly 'professionalism' could be a few hours later. It was a perfect summer morning. The countryside near Armagh is what people think of as quintessentially English, with rolling green hills, hedgerows and trees heavy with summer and crops near to harvesting; the kind of landscape exiles dream nostalgically about. Only this is a dream soured into a night-mare by over twenty years of sectarian violence, and the images of fear and hatred are everywhere. What appears at a distance to be a peaceful village becomes on approach a Catholic or Protestant stronghold flaunting all the paraphernalia of tribalism from kerbstones painted in appropriate colours to flags and graffiti proclaiming the virulent rhetoric of closed minds.

Driving along the A28 to Armagh I passed the Protestant enclave of Killylea with its ceremonial arch at the entrance displaying its loyalty to the crown like an unloved child desperately seeking attention from a parent that had long abandoned it. What I did not know until the next day was that as I drove along the road on that summer morning a Provo Active Service Unit was holding a family hostage on a farm up on the hill, and coolly checking out each vehicle below while they patiently waited for their target. I was driving over the land mine that a few hours later would kill four people, maim another and bring indelible trauma into six young children's lives. You soon come to realize that in Northern Ireland today it no longer seems to matter whether the ends justify the means, and that the violence is becoming an end in itself.

That weekend I left Armagh and the border country, frankly looking for some light relief. I was heading west for Croagh Patrick, the 'Holy Mountain' on the coast of Mayo. Every year, on the last Sunday in July, tens of thousands of pilgrims climb the mountain as an act of penance, following in the footsteps of Saint Patrick, who was said to have spent forty days on the summit in 441. In fact it coincides with the first day of the harvest and like many Christian festivals has pagan antecedents that stretch back into unrecorded history.

I arrived at the base of Croagh Patrick around Saturday midnight to find the celebration already well under way. Outside Campbell's pub at the base of Ireland's very own Mount Sinai, travellers were selling freshly cut staves for the climb while fast food vendors cheerfully undermined the gathering pilgrims' health. Come midnight and some hardy souls, presumably carrying a particularly heavy burden of sin, or – more likely – Guinness, were launching themselves into the darkness to climb the 'Reek'.

By eight the following morning the trickle of people meandering up the side of the mountain had become a stream and would soon become a flood as upwards of sixty thousand pilgrims from all over

Ireland converged for the last great pilgrimage of its kind in Western Europe.

Assuming the staves were for the aged and the infirm, I bought one anyway as a souvenir. Who was I kidding? It turned out to be the best fifty pence I ever spent. A few steps up the path to eternal salvation the heavens opened and a heavy wind drove mist and rain across the mountain's slopes. Ahead of me pilgrims circled around an understandably smug-looking statue of Saint Patrick before heading onwards and upwards into a low cloud. The climb is in three sections and I hit the pain barrier half way up the first, a rock-strewn nightmare of a path riddled with erosion channels already filling with muddy torrents. 'Do not climb this mountain in mist or rain' said a redundant sign by the edge of the path. As I paused for breath a little old lady cruised by, flashed me an encouraging smile and disappeared into the mist ahead. Someone somewhere was trying to tell me something. Twenty minutes later the message was coming through loud and clear as I staggered on to the saddle of the ridge with legs turned to Jello and lungs like a furnace.

'You are knackered,' said a small still breathless voice.

Still, the worst was over. The path ran on ahead passing, at the eastern end of the saddle, the first penitential station. Around it trundled the pilgrims making their obligatory seven circuits as they mumbled seven Paternosters and seven Ave Marias. As I paused yet again to mumble something less exalted a group in bare feet ambled by chanting the new Irish national anthem – Ole! Ole! Ole! Ole! Either the Irish are closet keep fit fanatics or the spirit really does move, if not the mountain, then certainly some people who climb it. The Leacht Mhionnain station was the point where Patrick was supposed to have finally cast the demons who plagued him into the loch below, and if he felt anything like me, I'm not at all surprised. All along the route groups of Cross of Malta and mountain rescue people kept a wary eye on the pilgrims. Every year brings a catalogue of heart attacks, broken limbs and even the occasional death. Alongside the path large stones spelled out the names of favourite saints: Patrick, Kevin, Benignus,

Sod this for a game of soldiers

Acid. Acid? Whatever it takes, I suppose, to get you through a dark night of the soul.

I decided to get a grip on myself when a one-legged Vietnamese woman hopped by and disappeared into the throng surging ahead of me to the western end of the saddle. After all, the path was now reasonably level and firm. With luck I would be down again in time for a late breakfast. Rounding a bend, all thoughts of breakfast, lunch, and probably dinner for that matter, evaporated. Above me towered a huge scree of murderously fragmented rock disappearing into the mist at an angle so steep that rocks dislodged by hundreds of scrambling pilgrims above cascaded down on to the pilgrims struggling below. So much for light relief!

It's called St Patrick's path and I was beginning to see why they canonized him. The next half hour was the longest in my entire life as I hauled myself up the unstable scree with the stave, dodging lethal rocky missiles and wondering if my knees belonged to someone else. The mist closed in, rain slashed across the mountain and an old man, scrambling by with the agility of a mountain goat, warbled: 'Thank the Lord for His blessing of holy water.' I suddenly thought of another use for the stave.

A man clutching an open umbrella did a Mary Poppins off the edge of the scree to the cheers of several big bare-footed lads dressed only in running shorts. As a rescue team moved in to retrieve him I noticed the little old lady seated on a rock eating a Mars bar. 'Not too tough after all, hey?' I thought uncharitably. As I crawled past she beamed me another encouraging smile.

'I always stop here,' she said. 'You get such a lovely view when it's clear.'

Up ahead of me the Vietnamese woman pogoed her way into the clouds as I heaved and slid two steps forward and one step back to the top. Sod this for a game of soldiers. And then, suddenly, it was all over. I found myself standing on the summit: sodden, dripping with sweat, hyperventilating and with trembling legs that seemed to be going in several directions at the same time. Around me on the flat stony area covering the summit of the cone, crowds of people as if out for a Sunday stroll perambulated another seven times around the second penitential station – the Bed of Patrick – before attending

Croagh Patrick: a vision from the Day of Judgment

Mass and circulating eleven times around the Oratory.

As is the way with mountains, the weather suddenly cleared and the whole of Donegal Bay and most of Mayo and Connemara appeared stretched out below like an hallucination. That was one thing about Irish saints: they had a great eye for the scenery. Behind me, like a scene from Bosch, pilgrims continued to struggle up the scree and the line of people stretched away down the mountain to the starting point almost two miles and over two thousand feet below.

Standing there exhausted and exhilarated, I was reminded of how all the major world religions cleverly exploited basic psychology to provide a temporary approximation of spiritual ectasy. Meanwhile, the priests sheltering in the glass box of the pulpit outside the Oratory hammered home the point.

'Life is a struggle, filled with pain and suffering. But struggle we must as we have struggled up Croagh Patrick today, as an

expression of our willingness in our daily lives to struggle upwards to redemption.'

No wonder this pilgrimage is so popular. The combination of physical satisfaction after a hard climb and the promise of spiritual reward in the next life must be irresistible to the faithful. As I found my own particular redemption from pain and suffering at the refreshment stall the weather closed in again, and while the pilgrims queued for confession the priest ended another Mass with a little proverb.

'And let us remember the story of the man with no shoes who despaired . . . until he met the man with no feet.'

There was a huge clap of thunder as the rain swept in and, right on cue, the Vietnamese woman appeared from a confessional booth and hopped through the crowd, which parted like the Red Sea.

If going up was bad, going down was far worse. The heavy rain and countless feet had made the scree dangerously unstable. As the penitents toiled upwards the shriven exultantly scrambled down. Time and again the rescue teams hauled battered, bloodied but entirely unbowed pilgrims to safety as mini-avalanches took their toll. Meanwhile the lower section had become a giant mud slide as the erosion channels turned into streams but still they came, chattering, laughing, urging each other upwards into the clouds and the purgatory of the scree that lay beyond. As I finally reached the starting point by the road I looked back. Like a vision from the Day of Judgment, a huge column of people streamed off up into the clouds.

I didn't know whether to laugh or cry. Ireland.

The struggle for redemption reaches a peak

10

Caught by the Short and Curlies

Returning to Donegal, I envisaged the unfolding of a touching little scene of reconciliation with the Incorrigibles. I would stride down the path to the cottage, fling open the door and call 'I'm home!' Fond felines, the anguish and trauma of separation behind them, would rush forward purring with delight at the joyful reunion . . . yes. The door opened to reveal two overfed comatose cats sprawled extravagantly in front of the hearth and apparently auditioning for a real peat fire advert. As I yelled 'I'm home!' for the third time, Cheesy opened one eye briefly before total apathy overwhelmed her yet again.

'Remember me? We recently spent five months together in the back of a Ford Transit. Very recently.'

Pugwash gave his legs a stretch without opening his eyes, and resumed his existential position – the one that says life is but a dream and people merely players of little significance.

'The one,' I continued, reaching for a tin of cat food, 'who usually feeds you?'

Two fond felines, the anguish and trauma of separation behind them, rushed forward purring with delight at the joyful reunion.

If nothing else, cats are pragmatists.

Meanwhile, life on the other side of the border in Northern Ireland had continued in its own inimitable way. I had met several people who were clearly their own inventions, and the perennial name games which provided useful clues to anyone's tribal and political allegiances had left me ever more confused and disorientated. What was Ireland to me was the Twenty-six Counties of the Republic to a Catholic and Eire or Southern Ireland to a Protestant. Northern Ireland is either the

The Incorrigibles express delight at my return

Six Counties or Ulster depending on which foot you kick with and just to put the tin lid on things my temporary base in Donegal was in Southern Ireland and further north than almost anywhere else in Northern Ireland. And if naming the part did nothing for clarification, moving backwards and forwards over the border did a great deal to heighten the illusion that I was in somebody else's movie, where other people's fantasies insisted on becoming my reality.

During the hot weather, I discovered a perfect spot: a grassy bank under a willow tree gently sloping towards a clear, deep, meandering river, well away from any road and devoid of human habitation. After a swim I fell asleep on the bank and woke up to find a tall gaunt man standing nearby, eyes clenched shut, mumbling. Despite the heat he wore a tight dark suit and a long mac. As I reached for the towel to cover the beginnings of an all-over tan, he suddenly opened his eyes and gave me a fixed grin.

'Have you been saved?'

'Sorry?'

The fixed grin took on the rigidity of rigor mortis as he stared at the towel.

'You can hide the flesh, but can you hide the sin the flesh is heir to?'

'Well . . .' I temporized as I slowly reached for scattered clothes. It was definitely time to put my shorts on.

'Have you been washed clean of the stain?'

His voice was rising. Either he was a man of the cloth or a detergent salesman.

'Washed in the blood of the Lamb?' he yelled.

It was the former then. Something I found deeply unreassuring.

'Reach out to Him, and He will gladly take your burden!'

I wondered how He was at untangling zips from pubic hair, the painful result of panic dressing. As I hopped about doubled over and desperately trying to extract myself from the metal jaws of the fastener, he reached a climax.

'You can run but you cannot hide!'

In the circumstances, I was unlikely to do either, given I was hobbling backwards at the time. Suddenly he held up one hand, palm outwards, closed his eyes and began mumbling again. I sneaked guiltily (and painfully) away as this strange scarecrow of a man wrestled with various demons for my soul. Reaching the road, I looked back to see him standing there still, arm upraised, fighting the good fight. Ending up with sore parts from nude sunbathing was, however, the least of it in Northern Ireland. Wherever you go there is a prevailing sense that just under the surface, just around the corner, regardless of how normal everything seems, something strange and threatening and possibly dangerous is going on. And by all accounts, it frequently is. Having acquired the habit of giving lifts in Southern Ireland, where everybody from school children to OAPs hitches, I felt inclined to do the same across the border, with mixed results.

Giving a lift to two young women I couldn't help but comment on the irony of a situation where, in potentially one of the most dangerous areas in Western Europe, people everywhere freely hitched rides. They were as pragmatic as the Incorrigibles.

'If you waited for a bus round here, you'd wrinkle up before it came by.'

I told them that in England now women never hitched alone and children were always counselled not to. Neither woman thought the custom risky.

'Everybody knows everybody else down this way,' they said, and went on to give me a running commentary on the places along the way where this intimate knowledge of each other's movements had resulted in various acts of good neighbourliness from kneecapping to murder to a mere hijacking. Violence in Northern Ireland runs parallel with most people's lives, and I suppose one way of surviving the stress of living with it on a daily basis is to separate it out from your own experience. Listening to the young women chatter on about the highlights of sectarian violence with a mixture of excitement and anxiety that was becoming familiar, I wondered how long you had to live in such an environment before you either developed a thick carapace of protective cynicism and black humour – 'Semtex – Ozone Friendly' read the ghetto graffiti – or got out.

I dropped the women near their disco in Armagh and headed for Crossmaglen to see another popular blood sport. Ireland's self-styled 'King of the Tinkers', Denis McGinley from Ballinasloe in the Republic, was defending his title with bare knuckles against challenger Dan

Rooney, who claims to be Britain's 'King of the Travellers'. It was a long-anticipated bout, billed as a grudge match, and attracting hundreds of travellers from both sides of the border. As with the English version of such fights, the situation tends to be highly volatile and warring rival factions are inclined to upstage the main event with colourful battles of their own. Publicans in the area wisely kept their doors shut and the police suddenly discovered pressing engagements elsewhere as crowds gathered for the bout. A makeshift area was roped off, the watchers pressed in on all sides and the two men stepped into the 'ring'. A great snarling roar of approval greeted each of them and warned off the other faction as the combatants briefly shook hands and glared at each other. Seconds later they rushed together with fists flying and for the next fifteen minutes pandemonium reigned as they proceeded to demolish each other's heads.

Within five minutes both men were unrecognizable, sustaining cuts around the eyes alone that would have stopped even the most vicious boxing bout. Blood poured down their chests and spattered the nearest onlookers as they pounded each other in a blind fury while the crowd became that strangest and most frightening of all things, a mob. A mob with one voice that yelled and groaned and screamed abuse from the first blow to the last. I looked around. Every man, and they were all men, stood rigid with tension, eyes sightless with rage, mouths open as they kept up the continuous roar. Whatever their original motives for being there, they were now a hair trigger from involving themselves in violence, and meanwhile urged their alter-egos on to ever more self-destruction.

It seemed impossible that the two men could survive such battering for more than a short time, and yet it was a good quarter of an hour before a group of McGinley's supporters rushed in and caught their hero, now fighting blind, and the fight was stopped. The crowd proclaimed Rooney the winner and he was paraded through the streets like a cross between a conquering hero and a blood sacrifice for the clan, which I suppose in a way he was. As I left, the battered blinded McGinley was still defiantly proclaiming himself the king and the talk was of a rematch in October. In one day I had come across three men who had not only created myths of themselves, but had come to believe them and, in the case of the travellers, persuaded others to believe in them too. And perhaps that was at the heart of the sectarian violence. When people are unsure of themselves, when the past is constantly resurrected – as it is in Ireland on both sides of the border – to explain the present, and when the future is uncertain, symbols and myths assume an importance which to anyone outside the situation may seem absurd or sinister. What gets overlooked is a prevailing need, even a longing, for something certain in a dangerously uncertain world. The crazed preacher, the two men who systematically beat each other to a pulp, all three possessed a mad kind of certainty, a belief in their own mythology. No more desperate, perhaps, than Orangemen parading in their tribal emblems and dressed like parodies of City gents, acolytes of some bizarre cargo cult, imbuing their masonic sashes and bowlers and brollies with the power to preserve a way of life that has gone forever. Meanwhile on the other side of the abyss the militants derive sustenance from the myths and martyrs of Ireland's troubled history to feed the leech of violence, and hardly a week goes by without new myths being generated, new martyrs created to the sound of the snare-drum of rhetoric that rattles emptily on all sides. As for symbols, the image

Acolytes of a bizarre cargo cult

of two would-be 'kings' beating each other senseless in front of a baying crowd would suit the Irish situation at the moment. Victims of their own mythology, passengers of circumstances and as blind and battered as the two travellers, the Militant Protestants and Catholics of Northern Ireland stand shoulder to shoulder slugging it out for an ascendency that no longer has any meaning.

It was a relief to cross over into Donegal and return to the cottage where sanity reigned in the delightful shape of a friend from Yorkshire, that ultimately pragmatic home county of mine where myth and reality were fused into one long ago. As we sat in front of the fire framed by a pair of shamelessly posing cats, the latest news of yet another killing on the border came through and elsewhere in the world armies flexed and postured and stood eyeballing each other, as armies will. Outside the wind was rising and rain beat against the windows. The television was switched off and the outside world receded. The Incorrigibles stretched and yawned and curled back into sleep.

'I think it's time we got you to bed,' said the friend from Yorkshire.

'Now that is the only sane thing I've heard all week long,' I said.

Opposite: myths . . .

and (below) martyrs of Ulster's troubled history

11

∞

Dead Ending

Life is a series of anti-climaxes, culminating in a disappointment . . .
So wrote that infallibly miserable bugger Anon, and as the mists
closed in and lowering clouds peed gently on Shercock, County
Monaghan, two well-travelled cats seemed inclined to agree. We
were on the road again on a final journey and my two infallible
barometers lounged sulkily about the van, peering gloomily out at
the rain and heaving heartfelt sighs. Clamp a pair of Walkmans on
their heads and they could pass for terminally bored adolescents. Not
only was the camper at the end of its tether, but so was an on-going
relationship that had survived the vicissitudes of Ireland's weather, the
day-to-day high tension of the border country, and several bouts of
homicidal tendencies initiated by a pair of nihilists suffering from an
illusion of central position. Not a lot had changed in that department,
and, as with the residents of Northern Ireland, it was surprising what
one could get used to. But like a partnership that had skated over thin
ice for too long, the cracks could no longer be ignored. In more ways
than one, we had reached the end of the road.

Shercock was a pleasant enough place. Plain, rambling, and unas-
suming, it meanders down the hill past the inevitable church to several
small lakes that remained invisible in the mist. It was the kind of place
that would inspire Steven Spielberg rather than David Lynch, with
an aura of rural simplicity tempered by an occasional oddness rather
than spectacular weirdness, although several weeks on the border had
taught me to hedge my bets. On a wet Thursday afternoon, only
locals pottered about, inured to the rain. The local churchyard, often
an ad-hoc community centre in such places, was almost deserted.
In it were two family graves, named after the maternal side of the

Terminal boredom sets in

family. The sole occupant, a gravedigger, intoned a litany on the local Connolly clan, distantly related to half my family. Shercock had been their point of departure in the mid-nineteenth century, as part of the great post-famine diaspora that eventually created both modern Ireland and an Ireland abroad.

'Ah, they've all gone now,' said our man, neatly anticipating my line of thought.

'What happened?'

'They've all passed over the Jordan.'

Which was topical, I suppose, if slightly bemusing.

'Why?'

'Because they're dead.'

Ah, that Jordan.

'Are there any other Connollys left in the area?'

'Dead, all dead.'

'What, all of them?'

'I should say so. They were never very much for living long, the Connollys.'

This will come as a surprise to several relatives of mine, all enthusiastically pottering through their eighties.

Following the trail of my wandering maternal predecessors after they left Ireland had eventually led me to Guernsey, where my great-grandfather had settled and married a French woman, Margaret. Between his long voyages in the merchant navy, they managed to produce six children, three girls and three boys. Among them was my grandfather Thomas, who, despite considerable opposition from his family, married my grandmother, Hilda May. She was a Protestant, and the result was a split between the two families that echoed the sectarian divisions of the border country they came from and still prevails in the killing grounds of Monaghan and Armagh. Perhaps the anger I felt over the bloody pointlessness of sectarian violence went deeper than I realized, and had its roots in my own family history. My mother was the first born of six children, and her paternal grandmother promptly put a curse on this innocent product of a mixed marriage, extending the long arm of prejudice to the unlikely setting of Hull. Glancing across at the Incorrigibles sullenly peering out of the camper windows, I wondered if such things passed

They've all passed over the Jordan

from one generation to the next.

'The last was Father Connolly,' droned a familiar voice.

Father? I did a quick résumé of some of my recent comments on the Catholic Church. Maybe the Incorrigibles were a form of divine justice, particularly Cheesy? A sort of mini-plague visited upon the ungodly. After five months on the road with her, the argument that Cheesy was actually an act of God was very persuasive. The voice of doom interrupted the flow of paranoia.

'A fine man. In Canada, up among the Eskimos, they say.'

Yes, that sounded like one of my lot. The tradition of wandering off and tilting at windmills was well established in the family: I was merely the last in a long line. Besides, more prosaically, two sisters of my grandfather had emigrated to Canada in the 1920s and returned briefly to investigate an old family legend of a fortune left in Chancery in Guernsey. It seemed on a par with converting Eskimos to Catholicism, although to this day the rumour persists, an unravelled strand of family history that stubbornly refuses to merge into the more familiar saga of the clan.

So, after almost six months and a number of adventures mainly instigated by a pair of nihilists in fur coats, I had finally discovered (half) my beginnings, only to find that, like most trips down memory lane, it was the travelling rather than the arriving that mattered. Here I was standing at my roots and all I had to show for it was a soggy T-shirt and the aphorisms of a walk-on character from a Beckett play. Surely I ought to be feeling a sense of continuity, links in a chain of being that stretched back into the Celtic twilight. Well, something.

'Loife,' anticipated the Albert Camus of cemeteries.

'Absolutely.'

As the drizzle settled into a steady downpour I wondered, not for the first time, if people chose occupations or occupations chose people. This man was probably the moving spirit behind some of the epitaphs on the gravestones. One in particular caught my fancy:

> 'Our darling Fanny Rabbet, was
> gathered very soon.
> 'Twas in the dewy morning, not
> in the glare of noon.
> Our saviour sent his angels to
> bear thee hence our own.
> To plant her in the garden,
> where sorrow's never known.'

Not too soon, I noticed, given she was eighty-four, although with a name like Fanny Rabbet I could only admire her tenacity in resisting a welcome early planting. Meanwhile the place was littered with people who unaccountably 'fell asleep'. Insomnia has its advantages apparently.

The gravedigger leaned on his shovel, gazed off into the rain, and sighed. 'Loife.'

'Are the pubs open yet?'

I was beginning to feel a wee bit tetchy with our man on the shovel.

He brightened visibly, sensing a freebie. 'They are, and we have several foine ones.'

'Yes, I thought you might.'

What place in Ireland did not? I left him leaning on his shovel, oblivious of the rain, still contemplating loife.

In the pub a young man with terminal acne pulled a pint of Guinness in slow motion, eyes fixed on the television and an Irish soap that made *Home and Away* look like *Hedda Gabler*. I asked him if he had known any of the local Connollys.

'I knew the ould man,' he said, eyes riveted to a scene on the box that involved a couple swearing undying love against a sunset and surrounded by a number of photogenic sheep. For no particular reason, several nuns wafted by. While I waited for nature to take its course, I conjured up an image of a kindly old man, contented and wise, a hard life of honest toil behind him, annealed by the weather and Irish history, made temperate by a vast adoring family, and above all with an infectious good humour in the classic Irish mould.

'What was he like?' I asked as the credits rolled over the couple in a clinch with attendant nuns.

'Connolly?' he said, returning to the planet Earth and switching off the set reluctantly. 'Aargh, he was a miserable bastard, never cracked a smile. He'd sit in that corner like a stone in a field, never a word prised out of himself, nursing a stout all night.'

I tried to rescue a few fragments of a disintegrating image. 'What about his family?'

'The ould man? There was no family. They all focked off long ago, and I'm not surprised.' Great. I didn't bother to ask if he was wise. With a CV like this he probably had trouble getting dressed in the morning. I consoled myself with the thought that after 130 years, my connection with local Connollys would be as remote as Ian Paisley's with the sacrament. According to the pitted barman, the Connolly farmstead still survived just north of the village. Maybe somebody there could give me an insight into my far and distant past. I discovered a fine example of a nineteenth-century Irish cottage looking like something on a postcard, in a setting which even in the rain looked idyllic.

The door was opened by a large friendly woman in a pinny and wellingtons: Mother Ireland herself. I explained my quest and asked her if she could tell me anything about the Connollys who used to live in the place.

'Not reely,' she drawled in a Roedean accent strained through plums and polished to perfection around a hundred dinner tables in Belgravia. 'We're from Orpington.'

Orpington . . . Why – not?

'On holiday. Such a lovely hise, but oh the weather!'

'Life is a series of anti–climaxes,' droned a voice as I trudged back to the van and two depressed cats. So that was that. Five months, several hundred miles, and the net result was a good soaking in the company of Orpington's answer to Lady Bracknell. Loife.

As I drove off into the rain the Incorrigibles mounted a protest pee in the portable cat litter tray while vociferously making the point that enough was enough. I was inclined to agree when, at the checkpoint on the border, I was given my first body search. I decided there and then, as the squaddie rummaged over me, that it would be my last. It was time to head south for the ferry at Cork, and, as I made the decision, the gloom lifted. Suddenly home seemed like a very good idea and besides, it would be nice to say goodbye to favourite places along the way. The Incorrigibles begged to differ but were out-voted by that old standby, the can opener.

'He who controls the means of production . . .' I reminded two cats who were about as impressed with basic Marxist theory as your average Lithuanian.

Back in Donegal, peace and tranquillity reigned at the cottage as Radar, my friend from Yorkshire, provided a domesticity unknown to a pair of travel-lagged cats, and, come to think of it, unknown to me too. Despite the spectacular mountain scenery and huge empty beaches, Donegal is the least visited county on the west coast, and watching the squalls sweep in from the Atlantic across the bay at Dunfanaghy, I was beginning to see why. Elsewhere the world took a turn for the worse as men in camouflage or grey suits postured

The Great Blasket, ikon of fertility

and manoeuvred, rationalizing depressingly basic instincts, while an oddly passive public looked on with a detachment that bordered on apathy. Indoors, life centred on meals and the fireplace, which lulled the Incorrigibles into a sense of true insecurity. These cats did not fall off a Christmas tree, even if their new-found friends outside seemed convinced I was Father Christmas.

Regardless of the finer feelings of the assorted felines, soon it was time to hit the road again for a last journey. Besides, I was rather looking forward to seeing the mysterious Dingle peninsula again. Ho ho. Because the ever-mysterious Dingle had decided to live up to its reputation by cloaking itself in a bizarre warm thick mist which shifted from place to place like a mischievous wraith. Mountains, headlands and entire beaches came and went, now bathed in sunshine, now lost in a swirling grey fog. Off-shore the distinctive shape of the Great Blasket appeared like an ikon to fertility, in the form of a pregnant woman lying at rest on a vast bed of silver against a sunset that seemed to suspend time. Little wonder myths and legends had always haunted this part of the world, and, standing there on the western edge of Europe with Radar, I too imagined a different world among the elusive shapes in the ever-changing mists: another reality perhaps to remind one that everyday life itself was stranger and more surreal than any ancient fiction.

Cheesy – stranger than any fiction – also had her moment of glory when a *Guardian*-reading Irish fan came up to the van in Dingle and asked for an introduction to 'the one which farted at the British Army'.

'Fame at last, kid,' I said to the flatulent one as she assumed her familiar travelling position behind my left ear and we headed for Kenmare. 'Just don't let it go to your head, OK?'

Another small hole in the ozone joined the miniature galaxy created over the months. Perhaps she realized that fame was no more substantial than a Dingle mist.

12

⚮

Keep the Home Fires Burning

'The good news is – we're going home. The bad news is – by ferry.'
Neither item managed to rouse the Incorrigibles to much enthusiasm,
racked as they were by the virulent Red Tide, scourge of local shellfish
and, via an inevitable food chain, two cats. Cheesy moped about with
a life's a bitch and then you die look on her face while Pugwash
appeared to have his mind on higher things as he sat meditating on
the cat litter tray. The human beans in this mini-psychodrama had
not fared much better. Radar had been blitzed by the drinking water
and was now intimately acquainted with the bathroom of the genuine
nineteenth-century cottage complete with genuine nineteenth-century
plumbing that I had hired for the final week in Ireland. Meanwhile,
having lost several pounds the hard way, I was now on a diet of dry
toast in a vain attempt to solidify recently liquidized insides.

The comedy of errors was not restricted to our own little group.
On the road outside, the formidable Englishwoman who ran the
local riding school led her string of subdued riders past the cottage
bellowing commands that rattled the windows as they all clattered
by in the autumnal light. Exactly why people who get involved with
horses insist on becoming stereotypes remains forever a mystery, but
this large brisk foghorn of a woman was no exception. Neither were
the people valiantly pouring cash into a delightful old Victorian pile
nearby. I had the feeling another dream was teetering on the edge of
a rude awakening as the lady of the house wafted about in a Laura
Ashley frock, matching pinny and big green wellies. For some reason
she reminded me of Madame Ranyevskaia in *The Cherry Orchard*.

As we stood by the boathouse overlooking the beautiful Kenmare
river and autumnal Caha mountains beyond, she chatted about her
plans for the place. It was to be a country house style hotel, the
boathouse a restaurant. The latter, renovated in a bizarre mix of

Cheesy: life's a bitch and then you die

styles, looked, appropriately, like something out of a fairy tale. The holiday season in this part of Ireland runs from June to September.

'When do you expect to open?' I asked.

'Oh, in about three weeks,' she enthused.

It was probably my imagination, but I could have sworn I heard the distant sound of cherry trees being chopped down as I walked away.

That evening I stood on the banks of the river for the last time. As if to make a point, the west of Ireland was providing the kind of evening that etches the place in people's minds for years afterwards. Above a carmine-tinted river set against the blue haze of the distant mountains the sky put on a display of pyrotechnics that photographs reduce to kitsch. There was the slight chill of autumn in the air and the last of the summer's swallows soared above the river banks of trees already subsiding into a final blaze of colour.

It was time at last to head for home, and despite the perfection of the evening I felt a twinge of relief. The landscape was remarkable, the people invariably friendly, the pace of life seductive, and yet . . . Maybe it was a feeling all travellers have in a foreign land, of something just under the surface, almost within touch but forever inaccessible. Reach out and it retreats, pull back and it advances, a strangeness that hides itself and then surprises you by emerging when you least expect it. Ireland disguises its mystery with familiarity. A (fairly) common usage of English and an almost identical currency are reassuring signposts. Only, like many of the road signs, they can easily mislead. The country is like a raft floating on a sea of contradictions which make perfect sense to the Irish and invariably confound the visitor.

The gregariousness is endemic and even extends to a body language that sometimes alarms as the customary eighteen inches of space beloved of the anal English in conversation is whittled down to centimetres. And yet the Irish are also the most private of people, rarely exposing deeper emotions to strangers and preferring to display them indirectly when appropriate public venues allow inhibitions to temporarily evaporate. Entirely free and easy with the authorities, perhaps as a result of several hundred years of British law-making that frequently marginalized them, they subject themselves willingly to the most rigid application of church law in Western Europe by a body of celibate men who impose almost medieval restraints on the most intimate areas of their personal lives out of the recesses of an inevitably suspect sexuality. Perhaps they feel a need for these spiritual minders to keep a check on their Celtic exuberance that they deny the state, because even today the rarest sight in Ireland is a half empty church during Sunday mass. As for the legendary drinking it is indeed, along with the (conversational) crack, legendary. Except that in my entire time in Ireland I rarely came across the kind of incident that has become a weekend ritual in most British towns. Perhaps your average Irish male is so secure in his ascendency he feels disinclined to buttress his insecurities with a macho display of tattooed muscle to the gallery after ten pints of lager. Or maybe the Irish gift of the gab just allows them to use words to (usually) tap dance elegantly around potential trouble. Despite all this and perhaps perversely because of it, I had mixed feelings about leaving. I felt at home and not at home at the same time.

Maybe I had come to Ireland too late, lived in cities too long and

taken part in and watched the daily street theatre of London too often. Six months away from them had increasingly revealed the withdrawal symptoms of an urban junkie. I missed the habit, the daily high of adrenalin that comes from just getting through the day in a big city. But like a love affair that for unfathomable reasons just failed to work out, I would always remember the country with fondness and wished it luck with future lovers. I never did find what I was looking for, but then perhaps what I was really looking for never existed, or at least not in Ireland.

The next morning two drowsy felines climbed grumpily aboard the camper for a final journey through the dawn to Cork. Scrambling on to the ferry with minutes to spare, we joined the throng of home-going families, several argumentative dogs and the human comedy that invariably accompanies a crowd of strangers thrown together and unavoidably detained for half a day. Radar and I passed the time making outrageous speculations about our fellow passengers, aided by her uncanny ability to overhear several conversations at the same time from ten paces – hence the nickname. Across the boatdeck a couple heavily into parenting changed shifts every hour on the hour, managing to avoid both conversation and eye contact with each other as they supervised their warring brood with clinical efficiency. Radar had them down as a pair of child psychologists in the aftermath of a failed second honeymoon. Judging by the body language, the first one wasn't too hot either. Ah, the joys of unrestrained gossip. Other shipboard entertainments included an escort of several schools of porpoises and another impossible sunset which brought the ferry down by the stern as the entire complement of tourists, distinguishable from the Greek crew by their sunless pallor, crowded aft to watch the closing moments of their holidays.

We docked in Swansea to the poignant sounds of police sirens which raised an ironic cheer from fellow city junkies and a pang of nostalgia in me. Having said a fond farewell to Radar and presented her with a litre of Southern Comfort to see her through the traumas of the new academic year, I headed for the motorway and London. Two

We left Ireland with mixed feelings

ferry-lagged cats, oblivious of the culture shock of arrival, flaked out on the passenger seat, echoing their original state on departure six months before. Elsewhere, not much else had changed either. Arriving in early morning London we passed lovers at a late night bus stop apparently trying to eat each other while ignoring a guy in a T-shirt with an acid house logo and nothing else dancing to his Walkman. Down Peckham High Street I ran a familiar gauntlet of an impending mini-riot as the police hustled handcuffed young Afro-Caribbeans into police vans on one side of the street as their friends stood sullenly on the other. All eyes followed the camper as I drove between them, still sounding (and feeling) like a World War Two landing craft. I made a mental note to get the exhaust fixed – very soon. And suddenly there was Brockley, stubbornly unchanged, the house apparently intact under a sickly neon light. Two sleepy cats tottered out of the van, sniffed, stretched and proceeded to case their territory as though they had never been away. While I unloaded the van a racket broke out across the square. An over-optimistic local moggy was being disabused of the wishful thought that Cheesy had emigrated.

The next morning a cheerful young policeman filled me in on the high points of the summer crime wave as we examined the forced bathroom window and place of entry for the inevitable burglary.

'I loaned the phone machine to a friend,' I said as we totted up the losses.

'Good job, mate. These days they tend to ring for a mini-cab, give them a cut and nick the phone as they load up.'

Nice to know the good old socialist principle of income redistribution is alive and well in Brockley. I just wish it wasn't always my income.

That night as I was about to turn in I heard voices in the empty garages next door. Glancing out of the window I saw two men with a bottle – winos probably. And then one of them lit the bottle. Perhaps they were drinking meths and wanted a warm drink for a nightcap. Seconds later there was a muffled explosion. Ever curious, I opened the front door and was confronted by a huge column of flames spiralling upwards from a burning car by the side of the house. As Pugwash and Cheesy sat on a nearby wall and basked in the unexpected warmth of a stolen car fresh, apparently, from a local bank robbery and fire-bombed to remove prints, neighbours gathered and took the opportunity to reacquaint themselves with each other, as neighbours do in London at such times.

'I haven't seen you since they set the garages on fire in February,' said one.

'No, I've been travelling in Ireland.'

'Ireland? Rather you than me. It must be like touring through a war zone.'

'Well, these things tend to be relative, you know,' I said as the firemen battled to prevent the car's petrol tank from exploding.

'You missed a fabulous summer, really hot.'

A resident of Brockley, about to be reminded of a local hierarchy

'Apparently.'

As the flames died down and we said our goodnights, I gathered up two warm and contented cats and closed the door on the evening's entertainment. As the television news brought us another step closer to war and the politicians manoeuvred towards the next general election, Pugwash and Cheesy, ever mindful of life's priorities, nose-dived enthusiastically into a late night snack.

'Tell me something,' I asked the Incorrigibles as they finally sprawled out in front of a less spectacular but rather more legal fire, oblivious as ever of a world on the verge of a nervous breakdown. 'What is it your lot know that we don't?'

There was of course no response. Perhaps they were asleep. More probably they were maintaining a diplomatic silence.